"M"   19.00

Hansen, Joseph

Bohannon's Country

Bohannon's
Country

Also by Joseph Hansen

Bohannon's Book (stories)

Steps Going Down

Brandstetter & Others (stories)

Pretty Boy Dead

Job's Year

Backtrack

A Smile in His Lifetime

The Dog & Other Stories

One Foot in the Boat (verse)

THE DAVE BRANDSTETTER MYSTERIES

A Country of Old Men

The Boy Who Was Buried This Morning

Obedience

Early Graves

The Little Dog Laughed

Nightwork

Gravedigger

Skinflick

The Man Everybody Was Afraid Of

Troublemaker

Death Claims

Fadeout

Bohannon's Country

MYSTERY STORIES

Joseph Hansen

VIKING

VIKING
Published by the Penguin Group
Penguin Books USA Inc., 375 Hudson Street,
New York, New York 10014, U.S.A.
Penguin Books Ltd, 27 Wrights Lane,
London W8 5TZ, England
Penguin Books Australia Ltd, Ringwood,
Victoria, Australia
Penguin Books Canada Ltd, 10 Alcorn Avenue,
Toronto, Ontario, Canada M4V 3B2
Penguin Books (N.Z.) Ltd, 182–190 Wairau Road,
Auckland 10, New Zealand

Penguin Books Ltd, Registered Offices:
Harmondsworth, Middlesex, England

First published in 1993 by Viking Penguin,
a division of Penguin Books USA Inc.

1 2 3 4 5 6 7 8 9 10

PUBLISHER'S NOTE
These are works of fiction. Names, characters, places, and incidents
either are the product of the author's imagination or are used
fictitiously, and any resemblance to actual persons, living or dead,
events, or locales is entirely coincidental.

"The Olcott Nostrum" and "The Owl in the Oak" first appeared in *Alfred
Hitchcock's Mystery Magazine* and "Molly's Aim" was originally published in
Ellery Queen's Mystery Magazine.

LIBRARY OF CONGRESS CATALOGING-IN-PUBLICATION DATA
Hansen, Joseph.
Bohannon's country / Joseph Hansen.
p.   cm.
ISBN 0-670-84942-1
I. Title.
PS3558.A513B63   1993
813.'54—dc20   92-50742

Printed in the United States of America
Set in Times Roman
Designed by Ann Gold

To Al Silverman

Contents

Introduction

Sometime in the mid-1970s, Playboy moved to branch out and publish books. The editors wanted a new mystery series. Would I write a background sheet on a detective protagonist (thoroughly masculine, of course), and outlines for four novels? The pay must have sounded good to me, because I did as they asked. The editors liked one of my outlines, but not Bohannon. I liked Bohannon, and wanted to write about him, so I told Playboy "No thanks," and I filed the project away until I found time to do something about it. So far as I know, Playboy never published any mysteries.

In 1982, I was in New York to promote a new suspense novel of mine called *Backtrack*. There I met the late Eleanor Sullivan, editor of *Ellery Queen's Mystery Magazine*. At lunch in the Oyster Bar on Grand Central Concourse we talked about writing. Didn't I have a story she could print? I reminded her that *EQ* had turned down "Surf" in 1973, at that time the only short story I'd written about Dave Brandstetter, my homosexual insurance investigator hero. The then editor, Fred Dannay, had written me that *EQ*'s readers "were not ready for homosexuality" in their stories.

Eleanor, one of whose many graces was her honesty, said the policy hadn't changed, but didn't I have a story without that element in it? I said I had. I hadn't really thought of "The Anderson Boy" as a mystery story, but when she saw it she wrote that she loved it, but—couldn't I add a sentence or two at the end to make the point of the story clearer? I did my best to oblige, but—the "sentence or two" turned into fourteen pages. Never mind, Eleanor printed every word. That story gained me my first and only nomination for an Edgar Award from the Mystery Writers of America.

Since Eleanor next reprinted an old story of mine, "Mourner," I concluded that she really did like my stuff and I'd better try to give her some new work. Without, of course, a hint of homosexuality in it. I remembered Hack Bohannon, dragged out the envelope marked "Bohannon Project" from its rusty file drawer, and wrote "The Tango Bear," which appeared in December 1984. I stole the plot from a novel I'd written in 1954, which no one had wanted to publish—the moral being, never throw anything away.

After printing a second Bohannon story, "Snipe Hunt," in February 1986, Eleanor grew uneasy about my 10,000-word length—she felt the subscribers to *EQ* preferred shorter stories, which meant more stories per issue—and handed me over to editor Cathleen Jordan, bless her, who printed "Witch's Broom" and four subsequent Hack Bohannon stories in *Alfred Hitchcock's Mystery Magazine*, where the subscribers seemed not to mind long stories.

Before going on, let me explain how I came to choose Hack Bohannon as a hero, and how I came to locate him on the California central coast. I was born in South Dakota and, until I was fifty, had never been farther east of the Mississippi than Fond du Lac, Wisconsin. Naturally, I love the American West. As a small boy, in my dusty little Dakota town, I hiked to western movies every Saturday afternoon—Buck Jones, Ken Maynard, Hoot Gibson. My first stories, written at age ten, were westerns.

Later, in the 1940s, I became addicted to novels by the likes of Luke Short, Will Henry, and Ernest Haycox, and I never lost the hankering to write westerns. I guess the Hack Bohannon stories are about as close as I'll ever come. He's an ex–deputy sheriff and keeps horses, his own and those of other people, for a living. He lives in wilderness, or nearly so, and if he's a bit far west for a bona fide cowboy, it's because I felt I must write about an area I knew.

When I'm lucky, a couple I've known since high school days invites me to stay with them in their house in pine woods up on the California central coast. It's colorful, dramatic country —the ocean to the west, in many places crashing against tall cliffs, the mountains to the east, slashed by rugged canyons. Cattle graze by the sea, horses along the ridges of the foothills. Sea lions roar and sea otters dive for abalone among the rugged offshore rocks, where cormorants and brown pelicans perch to dry their wings.

So when Hack Bohannon moseyed into my mind, there was no question where he had to live and move and have his being. Admittedly, the Bohannon stories make it seem there's a lot of murder and mayhem in that peaceful part of the world, and for taking fictional liberties with their quiet home place, I apologize to the pleasant, gentle folk I've met there.

In *Bohannon's Book*, published in 1988, the first five Hack Bohannon stories have a thread of backstory running through them about Hack's wife, Linda. After a disastrous encounter with drug smugglers, she is living, speechless, totally withdrawn, in a mental hospital. Only in the book's final story, "Death of an Otter," does she seem to recover. In "The Olcott Nostrum," the opening story of *Bohannon's Country*, Linda is once more living with Hack. But her recovery is short-lived.

So Hack's helpers at the stables (old ex–rodeo rider George Stubbs, young student-priest Manuel Rivera) and Hack's friends at the sheriff's office (Lieutenant Gerard, the bright, attractive young woman deputy T. Hodges, and Fred May, the public defender) are the only real regulars in the stories.

While I was driving around Bohannon's country one day with a friend, I was shown a large, abandoned Victorian-era ranch house. The gaunt mansion, with its peeling paint and dusty, staring windows, obviously had to be filled with generations of ghosts and memories, and it haunted me, demanding to be made the background for a story. Ultimately I stopped resisting, and "The Olcott Nostrum" is the result. I had never before used the well-worn story line of the search for a secret formula, and it proved great fun to do.

What I remember best about the writing of "The Owl in the Oak" is that I did it while learning to use a computer. Even as the amiable young legal secretary I'd coaxed into coming to my house to teach me how was putting me through the basic moves, I was rattling away at this story. She'd never witnessed a writer at work before. It must have looked easy, because she told my wife she'd like to do that for a living. Sensibly enough, she soon abandoned the notion. Actually, a house—or houses—inspired this story, too. A lot of little old spindlework houses in the town I call Madrone have been painted up and converted into boutiques. There are always stories behind such small ventures into business. A very different house, new and expensive, right on the beach, had caught my interest, too, and I made it the home of an important and, I hope, amusing suspect.

As to the whys and wherefores of "Molly's Aim"—sometime in the 1980s, a new, very well-funded magazine chain in the deep South wrote me, asking for a story for a special mystery issue. Since its readers were to be young women from eighteen to thirty-four, would I choose a protagonist in this age group? I did, exhumed a plot from an unsold story of mine from the 1950s, and sketched out "Molly's Aim." The editors found my mentally backward Molly repellent, so she went into a drawer. But I didn't forget her. And it crossed my mind one day—I don't remember why—that maybe it was time, with the story's secondary character, Hugh Henderson, to test that antihomosexual policy of *Ellery Queen* magazine. It was, to my way of thinking, high time it changed.

So I finished writing "Molly's Aim" and sent it to Eleanor, who hadn't been offered a story of mine in years. And though it was as long as any of my other stories, it got a quick acceptance. I was pleased, because it meant I'd broken down a literary barrier against me and my kind. All my writing life, one of my aims has been to make my readers stand in the shoes of strangers and know what it's like to be someone else—someone perhaps very different from themselves, someone they may heretofore even have hated or feared.

"Molly's Aim" is the only story in this book not set in Bohannon's bailiwick, though it's not that far off. It's a lost backwater where I once stopped on a trip in a friend's pickup truck to eat lunch from a brown bag, and watch magpies stealing food scraps from a pair of large, sleepy dogs in a tree-shaded yard. The sunburnt, silent isolation of the town, hidden away among empty, rolling hills, made me fall to wondering what life must be like for its people. The source of "Molly's Aim," then, was this lonesome little town, though the barn, called "Copenhagen," stood off a back road in Bohannon's country. Writers create their own geographies.

The notion for "McIntyre's Donald" struck me years ago. I don't honestly remember when. I kept it waiting because it wasn't the sort of story I normally write. But it remained in my mind. And at last, when Viking decided to publish *Bohannon's Country*, I thought I'd take a crack at it. I put maybe 4,000 words into the computer, then was drawn away from writing to tend to household matters. As I did this, I reflected gloomily that I couldn't write the story and must instead tackle something more in my line. But when a week later I read again the pages I'd written, I felt I'd made a good beginning after all. So instead of wiping the words out of the memory banks, I went on with the story.

To my astonishment, it almost wrote itself. I'd expected all sorts of problems. I met surprisingly few. In part, the answer doubtless lay in my having just written about aging in my final Dave Brandstetter novel, *A Country of Old Men*. Another part of the answer surely resulted from my patterning McIntyre after my gently heroic older brother, Bob. Last, I suspect some of the ease in the writing was due to that long incubation period when, without knowing it, I must in the back of my mind have been trying out directions the story might take—if ever I got to writing it.

Though I tried more than once, as I worked on "McIntyre's Donald," to include Bohannon, the story refused him. So I wanted the final tale in this book to be a true Bohannon adventure—and a genuine detective story. As any reader of this book surely knows, detective stories follow a formula. Simply put, someone has been murdered, an assortment of persons had motives for killing him/her, and the detective's task is to determine which of these suspects is guilty. To the degree that the writer can breathe life into his characters, lend reality to their surroundings, make their predicaments plausible, and the outcome inevitable, the formula will satisfy the reader, no matter how many detective novels he has read.

I have strung many books and stories on this framework, so when I came to write "An Excuse for Shooting Earl," I expected easy going. I knew the drill. In the event, I had a rough time. Commonly, it takes me three weeks to write a Bohannon adventure. This one took me six. I can't say why, but obviously in writing it's wise to keep one's guard up. That "McIntyre's Donald," wholly unlike anything I'd ever tried before, gave me no trouble, and the formulaic "Earl" proved a job demanding almost inhuman patience and determination, demonstrates the continuing excitement of writing fiction. The process never loses its power to surprise the writer, who then may dare to hope the result will do the same for his readers.

Bohannon's
Country

The Olcott Nostrum

The bare-raftered, plank-walled room, with its pine wardrobe and chest of drawers, rocker, straw-seated Mexican ladderback chair, braided rug, was no different this sunny morning from any other. Except that now he was not alone in it, not alone as he'd been for the past three years in the pine poster bed with its patchwork quilt.

Linda lay beside him, slight and soft and warm. Her honest beauty, quiet laughter, shining eyes had made life good again for Hack Bohannon. She drowsed now, after gentle loving. He slipped quietly out of bed and stood gazing down at her, in wonder at his luck in getting her back, and with an ache in his chest for fear she might not stay.

She seemed well and happy most of the time—with him, and with the chestnut colt, Penny. But though she never said so, he guessed she felt less than easy with Stubbs and Rivera, the men who lived here and worked for him. Also, she kept close to home, putting off reunions with women who had been her friends before she was hospitalized.

Three years ago, she'd been taken hostage by Mexican dope smugglers, beaten, gang-raped, half-drowned, and had after that night retreated into herself and stayed there silent, lost to him and to the world. None of it had been her fault, but she seemed to fear that her onetime friends would blame her, or maybe stand off from her because she'd been in a mental hospital for so long.

These things were clear to him and troubled him, but he figured time would take care of them, if only she grew stronger. But she was so sensitive. A dozen times a day he saw her flinch at little mishaps and her eyes brim with tears for hurts to strangers she heard about on the radio or read about in the newspaper. He wanted to protect her, but how did you protect anyone that fragile?

He turned away, picked up his watch from the ladderback chair. The time made him ashamed. There was a lot of work to do in the stables in the mornings. He'd always done his share until Linda had come back. Now, on too many mornings like this one, he slept in. He showered, took fresh underwear and socks from a drawer, put these on, and was kicking into his Levis when he heard boots in the hallway, knuckles on the door.

"Hack." It was George Stubbs, long ago a rodeo rider, now in his seventies, without whom Bohannon couldn't manage a day in this place. "I don't like to bother you, but there's a lady here wants to talk to you. Says Belle Hesseltine sent her."

"Thanks, George. Be right there." Bohannon flapped into a fresh blue workshirt. Behind him, Linda stirred and murmured in the bed. Tucking in the shirttails, he turned and grinned at her. She grinned back at him, tossed off the covers, sat on the side of the bed. Stubbs's boots limped away down the hall. Bohannon said to Linda, "That was nice, wasn't it? Did it give you an appetite?"

She laughed, pushed back her fair hair, stretched, yawned. "With all the food George serves for breakfast, I'd better have an appetite." She rose and stepped to him, put a light kiss on his mouth. "It was much better than nice," she whispered. "It was wonderful."

"I'm glad we agree." Bohannon picked up keys, coins, wallet, cigarettes, a scattering of kitchen matches from the straw chair seat, and put them into pockets. "George says I've got company." He sat on the chair to pull on scuffed boots and watched her move off to the bathroom. He loved to watch her move—she was so light and graceful. He stood, called, "I hope it's not a client," and left the bedroom.

Bohannon, a lean man of forty, six feet tall, with a shock of Indian black hair, operated stables up here in Rodd Canyon back of Madrone on the California central coast. He boarded horses for town folk with no place to keep them, and had horses of his own for people to ride. He taught them to ride, taught their kids. For fourteen years he'd been a deputy sheriff, but that had gone sour for him. He had quit, yet people kept coming to him for help and, unable to refuse, he'd taken out a private investigator's license. He favored horses over most humans, he liked a quiet life—but no man had things just the way he wanted them.

Stubbs, a vast white apron wrapped around his stocky form, worked at the cookstove that was a very old model of white porcelain panels and nickel plating. He was ruddy-faced, with a fringe of white hair and bright blue eyes under cottony brows. He turned as Hack entered the high-ceilinged kitchen with its massive oak icebox and pine sideboard, to call over the sizzling of bacon, "This here's Miz Genevieve Olcott. All the way from Vermont."

A neat, gray-haired woman sat at the big deal table in the middle of the kitchen, a mug of steaming coffee in front of her. Her tweeds, her small brown hat tilted just enough so as not to look prim, bespoke self-respect and no nonsense. What marred her perfection was an Ace bandage around one wrist, a Band-Aid on her forehead, and a cracked lens in her glasses. "Miss Olcott?" Bohannon gave her a nod, got a mug from a cupboard, filled the mug from the tall blue-and-white-speckled pot on the stove, took it to the table, and sat down. "What can I do for you?"

"I've had some unsettling experiences," she said crisply,

"since I arrived in California yesterday. I've reported them to the local sheriff, but he didn't seem interested."

"And Belle Hesseltine did?" Belle was a lean, brisk old M.D. who had moved to Madrone to retire and instead got busier than ever. Bohannon burned his mouth on his coffee, lit a cigarette with a wooden match, took the smoke in deeply. The first cigarette of the day was always the best. "Well, Belle's got good sense. What unsettling experiences?"

"Oh, it's such a long story." Genevieve Olcott looked around her as if wondering what she was doing here. "I mustn't take up a perfect stranger's time with it." She made to push back her chair.

"You can't leave now, Miss Olcott," Bohannon said. "Mr. Stubbs is a terrible cook, but his feelings will be hurt if you don't stay for breakfast. He'll sulk for days."

Genevieve Olcott smiled, but briefly, absently.

"Whereabouts in Vermont?" Bohannon asked.

"Ash Grove," she said. "I've been a schoolteacher there my whole life. I'm about to retire. And suddenly I received word that Aunt Nettie has died, and I'm her sole heir. The Olcott ranch. Do you know it?"

He knew it. Back yonder. Two thousand acres of sunburnt hills and valleys. Nettie's husband and her only child were dead. No Olcott had run the place in thirty years. Old Nettie had continued to live there, but it had been operated by tenants. Until the drought of 1976. Then the wells dried up, and the beef herds—white-faced Herefords, black Angus, cream-colored Charolais—had vanished from the whole region. After that, except for Nettie and a middle-aged couple hired to look after her and keep house, the gaunt Victorian mansion had stood aimless. The cattle business had revived, but not on the Olcott land.

"You going to live in the house?"

Genevieve Olcott smiled slightly. "Back in Ash Grove, when the attorney's letter arrived, I thought I might. A lifetime of

New England winters makes a woman dream sometimes of retiring to a land of eternal sunshine." She drew a quick, regretful little breath. "But—I fear I'm too old to make the change. It's so barren and brown all around the ranch. I'm used to forest-covered hills, with rivers winding through. Mr. Bohannon, have you no rivers here?"

He laughed. "Most only run in winter. We call them dry washes. But they're rivers, all right, when the rains come. Drown out the roads in these canyons sometimes."

"I had a different picture of California," she said.

Linda came in, wearing a turtleneck jersey, a little leather vest, jeans, boots. She worked in the stables with Hack, Stubbs, Rivera. She smiled at the woman at the table, but her eyes were wary. Bohannon introduced the women and fetched coffee for Linda. As she pulled out a chair and sat down, she frowned. "You've been hurt," she said.

"My shoulder bag was snatched," Genevieve Olcott said.

Linda blinked. "In sleepy little Madrone?"

"On the beach. I've taken a motel room there. And I was told that if I walked out early, I might see the sea otters feeding, sea lions on the rocks, cormorants and pelicans. And I did see them. Then, suddenly, I was pushed hard from behind. I sprawled"—she touched the Band-Aid—"and struck my head on a rock. I must have been unconscious for a moment, then I saw a man scrambling up the bluff with my shoulder bag, jumping into a car, and speeding off." She held up a hand ruefully. "I also sprained a wrist and broke my glasses."

"Did you report this?" Linda asked.

"The motel manager phoned the sheriff for me. Then she bundled me into her own car and drove me to Dr. Hesseltine's. When I told the doctor the sheriff hadn't seemed interested in my earlier reports, she insisted I come here."

George Stubbs limped to the table with a platter covered by a napkin, from under which steam wisped. He set the platter in the center of the table, and a small plate holding a slab of butter. Bohannon helped him fetch eating plates loaded with fried potatoes, eggs, Canada bacon. Both men took chairs, and Stubbs uncovered the platter.

"Sourdough biscuits," he said. "Help yourself."

When they'd finished eating, Bohannon rocked back his chair and said, "What were the earlier incidents?"

"Delicious, Mr. Stubbs," Genevieve Olcott said.

Stubbs's already rosy face grew rosier. "Plain old chuck-wagon fare," he said. "But I guess you don't get that much back in Vermont."

"And that's regrettable." She touched her mouth with a napkin, laid the napkin down, turned seriously to Bohannon. "The first concerned the ranch. I'd gone to see Nettie's attorneys as soon as I arrived, and they gave me the keys and suggested I go see the place. I have a rental car. I drove out there." Her smile was bleak. "I can't say I was attracted. It's such a gray old house, isn't it?"

"It always looked lonely to me," Linda said. "Deserted, though I knew it wasn't. As if the heart had gone out of it. It needed—oh, children, chickens pecking in the yard, horses, ranch hands, kitchen clatter. It was like a faded old photograph—meaning nothing to anyone anymore."

Bohannon heard a tremor in her voice, saw that her eyes were damp. Why? Everything that touched her seemed to bruise her. He wished he knew what to do about that. All he knew was to give her love and kindness—an easy prescription, since it was all he wanted to do. Easy—but enough? Now Genevieve Olcott spoke, and in her gentle eyes was the same puzzled concern as his.

"I felt that way, too," she said, "and of course now it is deserted. The couple who cooked and tended to things stayed on while Aunt Nettie was in the Villa Descanso, the nursing home—she insisted she'd go back. But when she died, the lawyers let them go." She twitched a smile at herself. "When I got out of the car, a tumbleweed blew past. I felt as if I were in a western movie, in front of that tall old house, built on empty land a century ago."

"No tumbleweeds in Vermont?" Stubbs was amazed.

"This was the first I'd ever seen, except in films. I let myself into the house and walked through, remembering things from Nettie's letters. But generations have come and gone, haven't they? The old remember the far past best—or so I read. And though it's been kept up, the house is much changed. I saw it all, even the attic." She looked grimly at Bohannon. "Shocking. Someone had been there. Trunks were overturned, contents flung about—lovely old clothes, lace curtains, tablecloths, pillowcases. Crates had been broken into—of china, silver, cutlery."

"Oh no," Linda said.

"Sounds like kids," Bohannon said.

"I don't think so." Genevieve Olcott's headshake was firm. "No—someone had searched for something. Hurriedly, but thoroughly. Storage cabinets had been pried open, old papers and photographs scattered. Books had been swept off shelves onto the floor. There was a table with test tubes and retorts, all hung with cobwebs. My cousin Gordon's, I suppose. He was a doctor. The drawers had all been pulled out and dropped. There was nothing in them but dust."

Linda shivered. "Weren't you frightened?"

"I was too angry for that," Genevieve Olcott said. "Outraged. To think that these lovely old things, so carefully packed away, treasured for so long, had been treated so brutally. I picked up an enormous old hat, white straw and netting, the crown wrapped in egret plumes, surely from before the first war. I stood there dreaming of who might have worn it and when—and I heard a car door slam below.

"I wondered who was coming. One of Nettie's attorneys, I supposed. Who else knew I was there? I went to a dormer window, wiped away a circle of dust with my hand, and peered down. But it wasn't anyone arriving. It was someone leaving. In a little gray car—what do you call them? Hatchbacks? And in a great hurry. The tires spun up a cloud of dust, the engine roared, and the car veered from side to side, as if the driver were in a panic to get away."

Linda was pale. "He'd been in the house with you."

"Wonder how you missed meeting on the stairs." Stubbs rose to collect the empty plates and carry them to the sink. Silver and china rattled, water splashed. "He must have been surprised as you that anybody'd come out there."

"You were looking out a rear window," Bohannon said. "That's why you hadn't seen the car when you arrived."

"True. I—" Genevieve Olcott's mouth dropped open. A thought had surprised her. "Why, do you know—I believe that was the same car the man drove this morning, the one who stole my purse. A gray hatchback with a thin red stripe."

Bohannon gave her a smile. "Good for you. All right—you reported the vandalism in the ranch attic. Then what?"

"Then the same thing happened to my motel room. Can you imagine it? While I was in San Luis Obispo, attending Nettie's funeral—which was, of course, my real reason for flying all the way out to California."

"Must've been a big funeral," Stubbs called from the sink. "Oldest living inhabitant. There was big, long write-ups in all the papers. Here, L.A., San Francisco."

"She was a wonderful old woman, a living history book. Her handwriting was shaky, of course, but her letters were marvelous. About her days here as a young woman."

"Sheriff didn't care your room had been tossed?"

"It's a common crime," she said. "So they told me."

"That's a fact," Bohannon said, "but I'm not much of a believer in coincidence. It figures the same fellow who rifled the attic searched your room, and then decided this valuable thing he's in such a sweat to lay hands on must be in your purse." He set the empty coffeepot on the table, took his chair again, lit another cigarette. "What is it, Miss Olcott?"

She shook her head. "I can't imagine."

Bohannon scowled, scratched his head, tilted his chair back

again. "He had reason to think it was in the attic. He couldn't find it. You appeared. He figured you knew where it was hidden. That Nettie's lawyers had told you, that it was in Nettie's will."

"But they didn't," she said. "It wasn't."

"Well, we know one thing for sure"—Stubbs used a white-handled brush with green plastic bristles to scrub plates—"it ain't gold bars or anything big and heavy like that. How come he didn't jump Miss Olcott there at the ranch house and take it off her, Hack? How come he hightailed it out of there like he done?"

"Good question," Bohannon said, and to Genevieve Olcott, "The man who knocked you down on the beach—what did he look like? You said you got a glimpse of him."

"Stocky," she said. "Middle-aged or old. Medium height. But I couldn't see his face. He had one of those knitted ski masks pulled over his head."

"There's your answer," Bohannon told Stubbs. "Man didn't want her to see his face."

"But why?" she cried. "I know no one here. I've never been farther from Ash Grove than Boston."

"He didn't want to kill you." Bohannon twisted out the cigarette in the old square glass ashtray that lived on the table. "And he didn't want you able to identify him later." He pushed back his chair. "Excuse me, please." He went to the sideboard and picked up the phone. The number he dialed got him the sheriff's station. T. Hodges answered, the young woman deputy he'd kept chaste company with during the last months of Linda's illness. "Did they find Genevieve Olcott's handbag yet?" he asked.

"In a Dumpster in San Luis," T. Hodges said. She was subdued these days when she talked to him. But she still did talk to him, and he was grateful for that. He liked her and didn't want to lose her friendship. He asked for the exact location of the Dumpster, and she gave it to him. "Hack, how is Linda? How's she doing?"

"Fine." He wished he was as sure of that as he made it sound. "I'll tell her you said hello." He threw Linda a smile, and saw an anxious look on Genevieve Olcott's strict, kindly face. "Everything all right with the purse? Nothing missing?" Bohannon asked. T. Hodges said there was no cash in the wallet. Bohannon repeated this to the schoolteacher. She waved a dismissive hand.

"There was no cash," she said, "only credit cards and traveler's checks. Oh!" She paled, half rose, reached out. "And my airline ticket. Is my airline ticket there?"

Bohannon asked, and gave her a grin and a nod. He told T. Hodges, "I think she wants to get back to Vermont."

"I don't blame her," T. Hodges said, "after all that's happened to her. We've been trying to locate her. She's at your place, is she?"

"Stuffed with Stubbs's biscuits," Bohannon said. "They'll charge her for extra weight on that flight." At the sink, Stubbs clattered plates, snorted, growled. Bohannon thanked T. Hodges and hung up the phone. He crossed the broad planks of the kitchen floor to a row of brass hooks by the open door. He took down his sweat-stained Stetson and put it on. "All right, Miss Olcott," he said. "I'll go see what I can find out."

San Luis Obispo is hemmed in by hills. You can see down any of its straight streets from one end to the other. It has a college, bookstores, and music shops, and trees grow along some of its business streets. One of those rivers Genevieve Olcott wondered about runs through it. It's a pleasant town, but fourteen miles from the ocean, it can get hot in summer. This was one of those days. His shirt was sticking to his back when he braked his rackety pickup truck in an alley beside a long, white-walled warehouse near the corner T. Hodges had named for him. The Dumpster was dented and scarred. He got down from the truck, raised the Dumpster's lid, and took a look inside.

A muscular high-school-age boy in torn-off jeans, no shirt, hightop work shoes, peered down at him from a loading-dock doorway. Behind him in vast dimness men moved and a forklift truck hauled crates. The kid was blond, with a flattop haircut and squinty eyes. He said, "The cops already come and took it."

"I know. Who threw it in? Did you see?"

"I'd have told the cops, wouldn't I?" the kid said.

"Maybe not, if you went through it yourself."

The kid stuck out his jaw. "I didn't. Why would I?"

"To see if the thief overlooked anything."

The kid's face reddened. "I'm not like that."

"Pity," Bohannon said. "There was five hundred dollars in the wallet."

"There was not," the kid said. "Just traveler's checks and cred—" His voice choked. He paled. "Oh, hell," he said, and turned to run. Bohannon grabbed his ankles, and he fell down. "I didn't take nothing," he whined.

"But you did see somebody throw it in the Dumpster."

"I only heard it land, and seen a car driving off." The kid tugged. "Let me go."

Bohannon hung on. "Describe the car."

"Honda Civic, gray, red pinstripe."

"Right," Bohannon said. "And the driver?"

"An old guy, gray-haired. I didn't get a good look."

Bohannon let go of the kid's ankles. He scrambled up and made to kick Bohannon in the head. Bohannon stepped back out of range. "This here's a loading dock, and these are business hours," the kid said. "Get your stinking pickup out of the way. There's a semi coming."

There was, rumbling, big as a house, silver siding glaring in the sun. Bohannon got his pickup out of there.

He went looking for the gray car. He rattled across the railroad tracks. He passed the old mission, its chalky walls almost concealed in cool, shadowy trees and shrubs and flowering vines. Straw-hatted tourists with cameras hung around their necks lined up outside the high wooden gates and read through sunglasses the gold lettering on a black signboard that told the mission's story. He drove on, up this side street, down that, crossing and recrossing the tracks. He came out at the railroad station then doubled back, taking east-west streets this time, glancing from side to side, moving slowly so as not to miss anything.

It stood on a patch of blacktop next to low, modern, sand-colored stucco buildings behind landscaping. A signboard tagged the place as VILLA DESCANSO. He frowned, pulled the pickup to the curb, sat with the engine running. Wasn't Villa Descanso the name of the rest home where old Nettie Olcott spent her last days and died? Yes. He'd read it in the papers, and Genevieve Olcott had spoken the name this morning.

He backed the truck up, and it shuddered as it always did in reverse. He clanked the gearshift again, and clattered into the grounds. An ambulance stood in the parking area, too, rear door open. Had it brought someone, or was it there to fetch someone away? There was a van with VILLA DESCANSO lettered on its side. There were miscellaneous passenger cars. And there was the Honda Civic hatchback. The slot next to it was marked with a doctor's name, but he parked in it anyway, got out, and walked around the little gray car. It was washed and waxed, and the glass of its windows sparkled. He bent, shielded his eyes with his hands, peered inside. The red bucket seats, dash, upholstery were as immaculate as the outside. He straightened and read the slot marker. R. DAHLTHORP.

He walked back and found the front entrance and pushed through glass doors into cool air that smelled of room freshener and vitamin B. He heard voices down hallways. Someone coughed and coughed. There was a thin strain of music from a radio. There were television sounds—hoofbeats, cracking six-shooters. A desk stood in front of him, fresh jonquils in a vase, a broad white telephone with many buttons, winking and pur-ring softly, but nobody in the desk chair. He touched the yellow and white flowers. Artificial.

A youngish couple, the man already bald, the woman too plump, led a curly-headed toddler by the hand down the hallway and past him, headed for the doors. "Gamma," the toddler piped, and tried to look back. "Bye-bye, Gamma." The man pushed the glass door open, and the woman dragged the toddler outdoors. From far away down the hall, a high, cracked voice wavered, "Bye-bye, Stevie." Bohannon saw a door marked PRIVATE behind the desk, and went through it. On his right a door stood open. REVA DAHLTHORP was incised in brown veneered plastic, DIRECTOR. Inside, a stout woman with short gray hair, a mannish blouse, sat at a desk and talked into a telephone. More artificial flowers stood on the desk, in handsome pottery vases. He took off his Stetson and stepped inside. The woman blinked at him, said something into the phone, and hung up the receiver. She started to speak.

"It's about Nettie Olcott," Bohannon said. He told Reva Dahlthorp what had happened to Genevieve, and the stout gray woman looked shocked. Bohannon said, "Miss Olcott doesn't know what this person is after. You cared for the old lady here for a year, and I thought maybe you could offer some suggestions. Something she said? Genevieve says her aunt liked to reminisce about old times."

Reva Dahlthorp smiled. "Indeed she did. I looked after her personally, you understand. It was hard to see how she could go on talking, but it never tired her, and it was fascinating. Her body was withering away, but her mind was quick as a girl's, and she remembered, it seemed, everything that had happened to her in her ninety-nine years."

"Nothing to explain what's been happening to Genevieve?"

"Nothing I can recall. It was mostly about times very long ago, persons long dead. Her father-in-law, who built the ranch, her husband, who ran it, her wonderful son. Brilliant doctor. Killed with his young wife in a railroad accident. Aged thirty-two." An ironic smile twitched Reva Dahlthorp's mouth. "She hadn't much use for our doctors here, I'm afraid. She kept saying Gordon was the only one who would have kept her from dying. He was a miracle worker, to hear her tell it. Never lost a patient.''

"She ever mention his laboratory in the attic?"

Reva Dahlthorp's face closed. "No," she said. "Why?" Bohannon shrugged. "It was the attic that got searched. Somebody thought something valuable was hidden up there. I wondered if it had to do with Gordon's work."

"She never mentioned it." Dahlthorp read her watch.

Bohannon said, "Whoever did it drove a car like yours."

Her head jerked up. She opened her mouth, closed her mouth, took a breath, smiled. "Cars like mine are common, Mr. Bohannon. There must be half a dozen like it in San Luis alone." She got to her feet.

"But not belonging to people close to Nettie Olcott," Bohannon said. "Or can you correct me on that?"

"The rest of the staff here—nurses, orderlies, therapists—work regular hours," she said. "Punch in and punch out. There are records of their comings and goings. There are none of mine. I arrive at about five or five-thirty every morning, and am ordinarily here until nine or ten o'clock at night. You are going to have to take my word for that, Mr. Bohannon. It's all I can offer." She came from behind the desk, marched to the door, opened it, and held it. "Now, if you'll excuse me."

Bohannon shrugged. "Thanks for your help." He gave her a thin smile, walked to the door, paused. "You don't know of anyone else who drives a car like yours? Somebody, say, who came here to visit Nettie Olcott?"

"In the last few days there have been television people, newspaper and magazine people, all sorts, in and out. It's been very difficult for us to get on with our routine here. A man called Wardour from San Francisco was a particular pest."

"Who did he write for?" Bohannon asked.

"He said he was a freelance journalist. But he was rather shabby, and always smelled of liquor. I couldn't make out precisely what he wanted. But his tape recorder was always at the

ready, and he asked questions of everyone he could corner—
even some of our residents, which of course is not permitted.
It wasn't until I threatened to telephone the police and have
him ejected that he finally left. Most disagreeably, I might say."

"Describe him for me," Bohannon said.

"Stocky, gray-haired, rather red-faced." She drew an impatient breath. "I'm really pressed for time, Mr. Bohannon."

"I'll go." He put on his hat, but he didn't go. "You didn't
see the car this Wardour was driving?"

"What?" She stared. "Yes, I did. That's why I mentioned
him to you. It was exactly like mine."

"I see." Bohannon nodded, tugged the brim of his hat to
her, and walked out of the office grinning.

The grin didn't hold once he was outside in the heat again,
rattling up the street in the old pickup. San Francisco was a big
place. All he had was a last name, a car model, and what might
or might not be the man's profession. It wasn't a whole hell of
a lot to go on, though he'd managed on less in the past. He
creaked the pickup to a halt at a boulevard stop, glanced in the
side mirror, and saw down the block behind him a gray Japanese
hatchback. Stopped or moving very slowly. The sun glared on
its windshield, so he couldn't make out who was inside. But it
wasn't Reva Dahlthorp. The windshield was dirty, and so was
the paint.

He drove on, and the car followed. He made pointless turns,
the car was always back there. He put on a sudden rattly burst
of speed, dodged into a dusty alley, parked behind a collapsing
garage, got out of the truck, stood in weeds, and watched the
little gray car hurry on past. Then he got back into the truck,
and now he was the follower. He did it better than the driver
of the car. The driver of the car wandered around for five
minutes trying to locate Bohannon, then gave up and headed
for home.

Home was on a tree-shaded street of old frame houses. The
stocky, gray-haired man who got out of the car did it carefully,

and walked as if afraid of hurting himself. He followed a narrow band of cement, climbed the wooden steps of a little stoop, and went in at a side door of a clapboard place painted green but not recently. Bohannon got down from the pickup, made a mental note of the hatchback's license number, then went to the door the driver had used and knocked on it. It opened right away. The man squinted at him with faded blue eyes. "How the hell did you get here?" he asked.

"I used to be a peace officer," Bohannon said. "I know how to follow people. What did you want with me?"

"Just to find out what you know about the Olcotts," the man said. "See, her lawyers said I wasn't to go near the niece, but she consulted you and I wondered what she told you. I'm trying to write a piece on the family."

"And your name is Wardour," Bohannon said.

"My name is Prettyman," the man said. "Robert Prettyman." He pushed open an old wood-framed screen door. "And you're Hack Bohannon. Come in and have a beer."

The place was one big room, kitchenette in a corner, a sofa bed, a chair that matched, a television set. No pictures on the walls but sheaves of handwritten notes and typescript pages tacked with pushpins. An old round dining room table dominated the room, littered with papers, file folders, manila envelopes, photographs, clippings, cassette tapes, a camera, a battered electric typewriter. Prettyman reached into a dingy little refrigerator and brought out cans of beer. He came at his cautious invalid's gait and handed a can to Bohannon. He set his own can down and, grunting, shifted books and magazines off a dining room chair so Bohannon could rest himself. Prettyman sat at the typewriter.

"Thanks." Bohannon lifted his can to the writer, and gulped down some of the beer. It didn't taste like much, but it was cold and wet and he was grateful for it. "You didn't tell Reva Dahlthorp at the Villa Descanso that your name was Wardour?"

Prettyman shook his head. "I always give my true name. It didn't get me anywhere. She guarded that old woman like a dragon. A mistake. A load of priceless history went into the grave with Nettie Olcott. It was Reva Dahlthorp who got Nettie's lawyers to have a restraining order put on me. I couldn't go near her, or any of the Olcott family." He snorted, set down his beer can, poked among papers on the table and found a pack of cigarettes. "Not that there are many left." He lit a cigarette. "Only Genevieve. And Wardour, of course."

Bohannon squinted. "He's a relative?"

"A by-blow. Gordon's kid by a mistress he kept in San Francisco when he was assistant to old Harry Duncan White there. Big society doctor. Millionaire." Prettyman picked up a thick file folder and dropped it again. "I've been collecting Olcott lore for ten years, Mr. Bohannon. There's a lot I don't know —but there's a lot I do."

"Sounds like it." Bohannon glanced around the room again. Bookcases overflowed with volumes, the name *California* in a lot of the titles. "You make a living writing on this part of the world, do you?"

"There was a good market in the sixties and early seventies. Magazines specializing in the history of the old West. I made money then. But it was a phase. Maybe the stories got too repetitive after while—how many outlaws' widows' memoirs can you print?" He shrugged, tilted up his beer can at his mouth, drained off the contents. "So I live modestly these days, don't I?" He grinned at the place. "And keep tracking down forgotten fragments of the past, and writing 'em up, mailing 'em out, hoping for the best."

"You said you'd worked on the Olcotts for ten years."

"Ten years ago I sold a piece on them," Prettyman said. "But I kept adding to the file whenever I stumbled on additional material. I'd be looking into this or that corner of history in this neck of the woods, and bits and pieces on the Olcott ranch would turn up, and I'd Xerox them and drop them into the folder. I talked to old Nettie once at the ranch three years ago, and she had a lot to say but nothing I didn't already know— except details. Then, when I got wind of this Wardour business,

I tried to see her again. But she was under Reva Dahlthorp's care by then, and I told you about that." He got up. "Another beer? Good."

"A man answering your description," Bohannon told Prettyman's back, "calling himself Wardour, even driving a car like yours, was all over that nursing home trying to pry information out of anybody he could. This would be Gordon's illegitimate son, is that what you're saying?"

"Could be." Prettyman came back with new beers. He stood blinking thoughtfully into the window light. "He was born about 1935, which would make him fifty-two by now. I never could trace him or I'd have asked him questions. His mother died long before I got interested in the Olcotts."

"Why would he hide?" Bohannon wondered.

"Provisions made by Gordon," Prettyman said. "When he settled money on Celeste Wardour and left San Francisco to return to the family ranch in early 1936. See, Dr. White had left Gordon Olcott not only his practice but half a million dollars when he died. Gordon could have had a rich life there, but for reasons nobody can supply he sold the practice and cleared out."

"Leaving how much to the Wardour woman to keep quiet and stay out of his life?"

"Two hundred fifty thousand." Prettyman sucked beer from his can, went back to sit at the typewriter. "I stumbled on the secret, really. Found out the name of Gordon's attorney from some source I forget now. His offices didn't exist anymore. I tried the home address. The files were there, all right, stacked in boxes in the garage. Place was falling apart. The daughter and son-in-law were alcoholics. They let me take the file on Gordon." He snorted. "What the hell was confidentiality to them?"

"They just let you take it?" Bohannon said.

"In exchange for a case of cheap bourbon."

Bohannon swallowed some beer, lit a cigarette, eyed Prettyman. "Two hundred fifty thousand was a lot of money in

1936, plenty to see her through and the boy, too. And all they had to do was keep quiet about him?"

"And never to ask for more. She signed an agreement." Prettyman found an ashtray, put out his cigarette in it, set it on a desk corner where Bohannon could reach it. "She never broke her word, far as I know. Kept her maiden name, lived quietly in San Anselmo, never married, died of cancer. When? Nineteen fifty-seven? Gordon's lawyer had invested the money for her, and she left the boy, William, well fixed. But I've checked official records down the years. He kept going into harebrained schemes and losing money. Inventions, gadgets nobody wanted. Then he just sort of disappeared."

"He's here—or was right after Nettie died," Bohannon said. "Poorly dressed and drunk, according to Reva Dahlthorp." Bohannon frowned, drank beer. "I wonder what he wants. If it's the estate, he'd be calling himself Olcott, wouldn't he?"

"His birth certificate doesn't name the father," Prettyman said. "He could take a flier at it in court, but I wouldn't give much for his chances."

"The day before Nettie's funeral," Bohannon said, "somebody tore up the attic of the ranch house. Somebody driving a car like yours. And William Wardour's."

"And Reva Dahlthorp's," Prettyman said.

"Somebody next tossed Genevieve Olcott's motel room, then snatched her purse and drove off in the same car."

Prettyman shrugged. "Not I. I've got a ruptured lumbar disc. I couldn't climb to the top of that house if my life depended on it."

"But you have been following Genevieve Olcott around," Bohannon said. "That's how you knew she came to me."

"Get her to talk to me. There's a book in the Olcotts."

"I'll try," Bohannon said.

"Thanks. Why the attic? What's up there?"

"Trunks of old clothes, barrels of old china, crates of linens. Books, papers, photographs. He went through it all and came up empty."

"Or she did," Prettyman said sourly. "Dahlthorp. I don't trust that woman. What was she afraid Nettie would tell me?"

"Good question," Bohannon said, "and here's another. Why did Gordon sell a fine medical practice to return to the home ranch and set up a laboratory in the attic?"

Prettyman stared. "Beats me," he said.

He jounced into the ranch house yard, and let the dust the tires of the pickup had roused settle before he climbed down. It was quiet out here among the brown, empty hills. The scattered oaks cast long afternoon shadows. He rummaged tools from the grit and straw and dried manure under the seat, slammed the door, walked past the side verandahs of the tall old house to find the power box at the rear. The electric company had sealed it. He used wire cutters to snap the seal and pushed up the handle, so he could have light inside if he needed it.

Boot heels noisy on the hollow steps, he climbed to the back porch. The sheriff had paid enough attention to Genevieve Olcott's report to come out and nail the doors up and tack warnings about trespassing to them. Bohannon pried the boards loose with his tire iron, crossed the porch, found the inner door locked, but had a skeleton key that worked on that. A new refrigerator and stove still stood in the gloomy kitchen, but cupboards yawned on emptiness. He crossed a floor of incongruously shiny vinyl tile, found an empty dining room and then the hall with its carved staircase.

The carpet on the stairs was reasonably new, so were the paint and wallpaper. And not all the furniture had been sold or stored in the short days since Nettie's death. Some rooms looked as if they were patiently waiting for their occupants to come home. The attic was as Genevieve Olcott had described it. She was good with words, as schoolteachers of her vintage used to be. But the windows were thick with rain-spotted dust, and he found a very old light switch and clicked it. A forty-watt bulb hanging from a twist of cloth-covered wire responded feebly. The test tubes and retorts on the laboratory table winked in their corroded metal racks.

Otherwise, the table was bare. Genevieve Olcott had put the drawers back, and he looked into them and found what she had found—dust. He took each drawer out, turned it over, inspected sides and bottom and back. Nothing. He stacked the drawers—there were three—on the floor, knelt, peered into the drawer openings. His heart bumped. He saw a dim white patch at the back of the center space. He reached in to touch it. Dry, crackly paper. His fingers found a loose corner and carefully pulled. The glue that had held it had long dried out. The paper came away. He got to his feet, stepped under the light, read numbers and letters in ink faded to pale brown.

He laid the paper on the table, went down a flight of stairs, and unscrewed a stronger light bulb from a lamp in a bedroom. He replaced the dim attic bulb and in the glare of the new one began a careful look around. Somewhere there was a safe. And in that safe was the prize the attic searcher, the tosser of Genevieve Olcott's motel room, the snatcher of her purse was after. A quarter hour later cobwebs clung to his face, his fingernails were grimy, sweat stuck his shirt to him, and he'd found no safe.

Hot, throat dry, he stepped to the rear dormer window that showed the clean circle Genevieve Olcott had made on the pane the other day. He pushed the window up for air. Grit crackled under his boots. He crouched and picked some of it up. White. Plaster? Mortar? He leaned out the window to breathe and under his hands the sill was splintery. Screws had been driven into it sometime and removed. At the center. To hold what? A block and tackle? Long ago. Dust filled the screw holes. He turned back and peered around the attic, wondering if he could have overlooked pulley wheels and ropes.

He hadn't. A man who'd take the trouble to remove the hoist beam outside the window after he'd used it wouldn't leave other evidence of his doings around. Bohannon pulled his hat down to his brows, lit a cigarette, stood scowling at nothing. Then at something. Chimneys ran up through the attic. He toured the chimneys, knocking on them, all four sides, with his tire iron. He was remembering the mortar dust. The backs of the chimneys were in shadow. He found an old mirror, wiped it with a shirtsleeve, held it to reflect light where he wanted to see. And he saw mortar newer than the 1860s mortar of the original chimney builder.

He set the mirror down and poked with the tire iron at the newer mortar. He pushed and pried. And a two-foot-square slab of brickwork grated open as if on hinges. Inside was a safe door with a shiny dial in the middle and fancy gilt trim painted on the black enamel. He went to the table for another glance at the paper, then worked the dial and turned the handle and pulled the door open. On one shelf stood little brown paper parcels of dried herbs and powders, marked with chemical symbols and Chinese ideograms. On the shelf below were piled three big brown envelopes.

Each of these was marked *Gordon Olcott, M.D., personal and private.* Bohannon respected that. He found a lace-edged yellowing pillowcase on the floor, dropped the parcels into it, the envelopes, left the safe door open, and the hinged-brick hiding place of the safe. He collected his tire iron, left the safe combination lying on the table, switched off the light, and went back downstairs and outdoors. There he laid the pillowcase on the worn steps and nailed the back door shut again. He picked up the pillowcase and, as he straightened, caught a wink of light from the ridge of hills to the east.

He stood gazing at the ridge until he saw it again—sunlight reflected off glass? A car window? He strained to listen in the stillness. A meadowlark sang. Did a car door slam? It was far off. What was over there? He knew this country. Nothing was over there except maybe a service road from the time this was a working ranch. Now a long trail of dust formed over the ridge and traveled along in the wake of a car he couldn't see. Prettyman's, Dahlthorp's, William Wardour's? He'd been watched. As he'd expected.

He pushed the tools back under the seat of the pickup, climbed in, slammed the door, started the engine. He laid the pillowcase on the tape-mended seat beside him. Those envelopes were the property of Genevieve Olcott. She must be the one to open them. But he had to admit to himself as he wheeled the rattly truck around the big empty yard, and got it out onto the road again, he was curious as hell to know what was in them.

A young man with a sunburn was behind the counter in the motel office when Bohannon walked in. The kid wore a blousy unbleached muslin shirt big enough for two of him and blousy pants of the same kind of cloth. The shirt was unbuttoned and not tucked into the pants. He was sunburnt on his upper body, too. Too blond ever to get a tan, Bohannon thought. He told the kid what he wanted to know about Genevieve Olcott.

The kid said: "It was my mother that ran out when she heard her yelp. Wasn't me. It was early. I was surfing. But when I got back, she showed me where it happened." He lifted a leaf in the counter, came out, led Bohannon outside. The phone began ringing in the office, but he ignored it and went out on the sand and walked along. Barefoot. "Come on. It's not far," he called above the noise of the surf. "If I'd been here, I could have caught the dude, maybe." Bohannon's cowboy boots made walking in the sand slow going. The kid stopped and looked back. "They find him yet?"

"They found the purse," Bohannon said. "Nothing stolen."

"There's the rock she hit her head on." The boy stuck out an arm. The wind flapped the roomy sleeve of his shirt, blew his long hair around. "And that's where the mugger climbed to the road."

The cutbank was twelve feet high, and almost straight up and down. There were rough places that would serve as handholds, footholds, but not for a man with a bad back. How about for a red-faced, middle-aged drunk? Or a soldierly middle-aged woman? Bohannon gave his head an unhappy shake, said to the kid, "Thanks very much. Oh, one more thing. Do you have a guest registered, name of William Wardour?"

The kid gazed at the surf. "Wheeler. No Wardour."

"Your phone's ringing," Bohannon said.

The kid shrugged. "We're full up." He moved off to let a foam-edged incoming wave wash over his feet.

"Maybe someone's trying to reach a guest," Bohannon suggested. "Wardour drives a gray Japanese hatchback."

"I check the names of everybody when I come on shift." The kid stepped deeper into the surf. His pants legs got wet. "You learn to memorize them right off. It's a trick of the trade." He looked at Bohannon suddenly. "Hey, that's our phone. I better get that." He ran off toward the motel. "Nice talking to you." He waved without looking back. "Let us know if we can be of any more help."

Bohannon laughed to himself, and crouched to examine the sand around the sharp rock where Miss Olcott had bumped her head. He found nothing. Out maybe two hundred feet a sea lion barked. Squinting against the glare of sun on water, Bohannon saw him on some rocks, a big fellow, yellow-brown, lazily scratching his head with a clumsy flipper. Bohannon went back to his pickup truck and drove up into Madrone. He parked on gray tarmac beside the sheriff's station where a tall hedge of old eucalypts rustled in the wind and dropped dry leaves and pods on the roofs of brown county cars. He pushed the pillowcase under the seat, got out, and locked the truck. The locks turned stiffly. He couldn't remember how long it had been since he'd felt obliged to use them.

He wanted to talk to Lieutenant Gerard, but Gerard was out enforcing the law. Bohannon got T. Hodges to coax the watch officer into releasing Genevieve Olcott's shoulder bag. Then

Bohannon took T. Hodges out for a coffee break in a little eatery with a screened front porch. It was their first real time alone together since Linda had come back. It cheered him up to be sitting across from T. Hodges again. She was uneasy about it at first, but soon she was smiling with her luminous dark eyes. It was her way. She worried that her front teeth stuck out, and unless caught by surprise, she didn't often show them in a smile or a laugh.

Bohannon said, "Linda's afraid her friends won't want her around them now, that they're leery of somebody who's been in a mental hospital."

"Either she's mistaken," T. Hodges said, "or they can't be much in the way of friends, can they?"

"They're all right," Bohannon said. "I know them. She's wrong. But I've given up trying to get her to phone them. It's no use, just upsets her. But she's lonely with only men around the place. Can you drop in now and then? Will you?"

T. Hodges nodded. "If you say so."

"Not if you don't want to," he said.

She looked at him meaningly for a moment, then turned to gaze off at the pines of Settlers Cove across the highway. "You're clever about your work, Hack, but you can be terribly dense sometimes." She looked at him again. Not unkindly. Gently. But directly. "Did you know that?"

"What have I missed?" he said.

"That I've fallen in love with you," she said. "Ah—Linda's very dear. I like her. I've nothing against Linda. But I know she's everything to you, Hack. And it—it hurts." Tears came into her eyes, her mouth trembled, and she pressed it tight and gave her head an impatient shake, angry at herself for letting her emotions show. She was a deputy sheriff, not some soap-opera weeper. And when he reached for her hand on the tabletop, she drew it quickly away.

"I never meant for that to happen," he said. "If it's my fault"—it wasn't his fault: there hadn't been a kiss or even a romantic word between them—"I apologize. I'm sorry. I won't ask again."

"I'll come," she said. "Of course I will."

Stubbs was raking the gravel drive when Bohannon pulled into the stable grounds. The white-railed training ring where little kids learned not to tumble out of the saddle was tidied up, so was the large fenced oval beyond and below it where older youngsters picked up the rudiments of jumping, barrel racing, show riding. Sprinklers watered flower beds. The shadows of the eucalypts were long. Bohannon parked the pickup beside the white and green stable building and went to help young Rivera lay down fresh straw in the stalls, fill water buckets, pour oats into each horse's corner bin.

When he walked into the kitchen half an hour later, Bohannon frowned. "Where's Linda?" Rivera, shedding his shirt, disappeared to shower. Stubbs hobbled from the refrigerator to the table with brown bottles of Anchor beer. A day's hard work told on his rheumatics. He suppressed a groan as he sat down. "She took Miz Olcott on a picnic. Put her on Mousie." Mousie was gentle and trustworthy. Stubbs read a battered wristwatch and glanced at the windows where the light was fading. "Time they was back, isn't it?"

"I'd say so." Bohannon had lit a cigarette. He took a long pull from it, and twisted it out in the ashtray. He tilted up the bottle and washed his dry throat with gulps of beer. He set the bottle down and got to his feet. "I'd best go round them up." He put his hat back on, sat down to pull on his boots.

"Where you been all day?" Stubbs said.

"I found what the thief must have been looking for," Bohannon told him. "In the attic at the Olcott Ranch. Hidden in a walled-up safe." He stood and stamped to settle his feet in the boots. "Belonged to Genevieve's cousin, the doctor."

"Not gold bars, was it?" Stubbs said.

"Not gold bars. Chemicals. And papers. That's all."

"When do we get a look at 'em?" Stubbs asked.

Bohannon went out. "When I bring Genevieve home here."

Linda was a good rider, but Genevieve Olcott was a question mark. How long had it been since the schoolteacher had been on horseback? Even steady Mousie could lose footing. If there'd been an accident, had Linda been able to handle it? Bohannon frowned and nudged Bearcat's solid sides with his heels. The horse rumbled a deep comment in his throat and picked up his pace. The solid clop of his hoofs went on and on. Bohannon followed the common trails, pretty certain Linda wouldn't try the steeper narrow byways with the older woman. He made sure to check every picnicking place beside the rocky, almost waterless streambed. No luck. Darkness was closing in. He winced up at the sky doing its customary color changes from blue to deep green to crimson. Where the hell were they? He drew breath to shout, and there was Linda riding toward him. Before he could rightly make out her features, he knew she'd been riding a long time. He could hear Seashell's heavy breathing.

"Oh, Hack, thank God!" Linda reined up the gray and jumped down. "She's gone, Hack. I can't find her. I found Mousie, but she's spooked, she won't let me catch her. And Genevieve's nowhere, Hack. I've searched and searched, called and called."

He got down and took the trembling Linda in his arms. She clung hard to him and wept. He stroked her back. "It's all right. We'll find her." Gently he stood Linda away from him, brushed her tears with his fingers, smiled into her frightened face. "Come on. You know tears can't help. Where did you find Mousie?"

She swallowed hard, worked up a wavery smile for him, and told him where and how. They got back on their horses and went to look. They found a sensible, low-heeled brown shoe in brush beside the path. They found Mousie, who had got over her scare by now. Bohannon took her in tow. They rode up the path, calling into the evening stillness, but only echo answered. Bohannon reined up Bearcat. "We have to go back. It'll soon be dark."

"But we can't leave her here," Linda cried.

"I don't think she's here," Bohannon said.

Linda stared. "What do you mean? You mean because she doesn't answer? She could be badly hurt. Unconscious."

"Maybe." Bohannon studied the shoe. "But the brush where we found this wasn't smashed down like it would be if she was thrown. I don't know what I mean. I just don't think she's out here, that's all. It's a feeling."

"It's my fault," Linda said. "I shouldn't have let her go on without me. I was laying out our lunch, and she said she'd just go on up the trail a little way and come back."

"It's not your fault," Bohannon said. "Come on." He pulled Bearcat's big, dark head around. "If she doesn't turn up, we'll ride back here tomorrow at first light."

It was dark and the stars were out when they reached the stables, where ground lights shone on the buildings. Linda looked pale when she slipped down off Seashell's back, looked as if she'd just about run out of energy. "You go on in," Bohannon told her. "I'll unsaddle here and join you in a minute." She looked at him with eyes filled with anxiety but she turned and obediently made for the ranch house, her feet dragging a little in the gravel.

As Bohannon undid Mousie's girth and hoisted the saddle off her, he saw Stubbs's thick figure charge out of the kitchen doorway. "You back?" he called. "I been getting some bad-news phone calls here."

Linda stumbled on toward the long board walkway where Stubbs stood. Bohannon put the saddle in the tack room and led Mousie into a stall that smelled sweetly of timothy hay. He didn't tend to Seashell and Bearcat right away. He knotted their reins to a post and went at a run to find out what Stubbs was hollering about. His boots knocked the porch planks. He put an arm around Linda.

"Kidnappers," Stubbs said. "They've got Genevieve. They're holding her till you give them the stuff you picked up at the ranch house today. They seen you, Hack. They know you've got it."

Linda gave a cry. It was a sound he hadn't heard from her lately, and had never wanted to hear from her again. It came from the deepest haunted places of her mind and spirit, where the old horror had dwelt so long. Hands covering her face, she dropped to her knees on the rough planks, then toppled to her side and lay hunched in what doctors like to call a fetal position. He thought it was the wrong word. There was no promise in it. It was a retreat from promise. He knelt by her, touched her, kissed her hair, spoke to her, shook her gently, but even as he did these things, he knew it was no use.

"What's wrong?" Stubbs said. "What's happened to her?"

"Hold the door open." Bohannon gathered her slightness into his arms, carried her through the kitchen and down the hall to the bedroom. He laid her on the bed. He was murmuring to her all the time, gentleness, tenderness. He knelt beside the bed and stroked her, as a mother will stroke a heartbroken child. But she didn't respond. His heart sank. He knew this Linda all too well. This was a Linda nobody could reach. She was gone again. He sensed Stubbs standing in the doorway and looked. The old man's face was rumpled with dismay and self-reproach.

"I'm sorry, Hack. I shouldn't have blurted it out."

"Don't blame yourself." Bohannon pushed wearily to his feet, all hope gone out of him. It had been a long day, and he was tired before this. Now it seemed almost too much to have to keep upright, let alone move to do anything. He snapped on the small lamp on the chest of drawers, though she wouldn't know it. Her darkness was too deep for any light to reach. He stepped out and softly closed the door. "It was the word 'kidnappers,' I guess." He patted Stubbs's shoulder, and walked back to the kitchen. "Phone Atascadero for me, will you? Tell

Dr. Manfredi what's happened. Then call Belle Hesseltine. She's nearer, she'll get here first."

While the old man stood at the sideboard, worked the phone, spoke quietly into it, Bohannon went out to unsaddle Bearcat and Seashell and put them in their stalls. Then he got Genevieve Olcott's shoulder bag off the seat of the GM and pulled the pillowcase out from under the seat. He took these things back into the kitchen and laid them on the table, where Stubbs had set a bottle of Old Crow and a glass of ice cubes. Bohannon poured himself a drink but didn't touch it. He got up, went into the sitting room, and took down his Winchester from above the fireplace where Stubbs's rodeo trophies gleamed on the mantelpiece. He looked at the room, with its flowered chintz curtains and furniture covers, Linda's choice, and turned sharply away. He stopped at the bedroom and looked in at her. No change. He hadn't thought there would be. Back in the kitchen, he said to Stubbs, "Rivera's back at the seminary, right? Get him down here, will you?"

Stubbs grunted that he would. Bohannon sat at the table and, in the light of the lamp that glowed in its center, emptied the pillowcase. "What did you tell the kidnappers?"

"That you wasn't here, didn't know when you would be."

"What did the voice sound like?" Bohannon slipped papers out of the top envelope. They were handwritten, a doctor's records, patient after patient, dates, ailments, tests, treatment. He couldn't make anything of them.

"Don't know if it was a man or a woman," Stubbs said. He peered over Bohannon's shoulder. "That don't look important enough to kick up all this excitement."

"Belle will know why," Bohannon said.

"I don't know if she's coming," Stubbs said. "I had to leave a message on her doggone answering machine."

Bohannon pushed the records back, opened the second envelope, slipped its contents out. More patients' records. He blinked at them in the lamplight, but he couldn't focus. "Is Manfredi coming?"

"Fast as he can," Stubbs said. "I'll ring Rivera now." He watched Bohannon drink. "You going to put away straight whiskey like that, you better eat."

"I'm not hungry," Bohannon said. He pushed these records back into the second envelope and opened the third. The contents of this one were different. He hadn't had much schooling. But he'd read all his life, every kind of book and magazine. It was a way of finding out enough to make yourself useful in the world. He didn't understand symbols and formulae, but he recognized them when he saw them, and they were what Gordon Olcott had scribbled on this paper. He'd leave that for Belle Hesseltine, too. He put it aside, and here was genuine writing, a stack of pages stapled together, the staple turned to gritty rust with the years.

Stubbs came from the stove into the circle of light at the table and set down a steaming plate of one of his favorite concoctions, turkey hash. He laid a fork beside the plate noisily. "Wake up and eat, Hack." He picked up a large ketchup bottle and made a show of cranking off its top. That roused Bohannon. "No, no. Don't do that to it, for God's sake."

"Well, eat it like it is, then, but eat it."

Bohannon hadn't taken any food since breakfast. He shoveled down the hash hungrily, and his belly was grateful. But his mind was on his reading. If what Gordon Olcott said here was true, then his formula was worth any amount of trouble to lay hands on. It had proved out on patient after patient, with illnesses from diphtheria to encephalitis to cancer. The only thing wrong was the expense. The formula was costly to make up even in tiny batches. Gordon had had to work out substitutes for some key ingredients—mostly Chinese imports.

The phone jangled, loud in the stillness. His head jerked up, he slammed out of his chair and was at the sideboard in two long strides. He grabbed the receiver as if to choke the life out of it. "Bohannon. Let me talk to Genevieve Olcott."

"She's all right. Just bring what you found in the chimney to

Schooner Point in half an hour. Come alone and unarmed. We'll turn her over to you then.''

Whose voice was it—Reva Dahlthorp's, Robert Prettyman's, William Wardour's? Damned if he could tell. Reva Dahlthorp was trained and conditioned to save life, not take it. Prettyman would have taken those photos that Genevieve had found still strewn around the attic. Wardour's character he had no way of gauging. Two out of three wasn't bad, but it wasn't good either. He said, "Someone's come in. I'll have to call you back. What's the number?''

"Don't take me for a fool," the voice snapped. "Just do as I say. This is a matter of saving mankind. The life of one little old lady scarcely matters in that equation." And the line went dead.

Bohannon dropped the receiver into place. Where was Stubbs? He found the old man seated in the rocker by the soft light of the lamp, watching over Linda, quiet and motionless on the bed. Bohannon lifted a hand to him, went back to the kitchen for the rifle, then out to the truck. He used the two-way radio there to reach a sheriff's car on patrol and asked Vern, the young deputy he knew, to check out a pay phone along the highway near Schooner Point. He sat waiting in the truck. Rivera found him there.

"What's the matter?" he said. "Is it your wife?''

Bohannon told him the story. Rivera's smooth, brown face looked as if all the world's sorrows had been poured into his ear. "I'll go see if I can help." His shoes crunched away across the gravel. He was wearing a cassock. Bohannon frowned. It wouldn't be long before the kid became a priest. He'd miss him. The radio crackled and a scratchy voice said, "Don't see anybody around that phone, Hack.''

"Thanks," Bohannon said. "Just a crank call, I guess." He twisted the key in the ignition and the starter whinnied and the engine clattered into life. He ground the gears into reverse, reached for the hand brake, and headlights swept the pickup. Belle Hesseltine's handsome new bangwagon swung in beside him, stopped, the skinny old woman climbed down. The cool night breeze fluttered her cropped white hair. She pushed at her hair with a bony hand and squinted at him.

"Where you going? Forget you invited me here, did you?"

"No." He switched off the engine, jumped down, took her elbow, walked her briskly toward the ranch house, explaining about Linda on the way. They went straight to the bedroom. The old doctor sat on the edge of the bed, opened her kit, looked at Stubbs, who got up quickly from the rocker, and at Rivera standing looking worried at the foot of the bed. "You men get out of here," she said. "I'll be along in a minute."

"Something I want your help with," Bohannon said.

In the kitchen, Stubbs rattled at the stove, making coffee. "That old gal scares me. Always makes me feel like a little kid she caught smoking out behind the barn."

"She takes us all that way." Bohannon stood at the table, looked at the whiskey bottle, left it alone. He read his watch. Ten minutes had passed since the phone call. He couldn't get to Schooner Point on time now if he had a racing car. He lit a cigarette with shaky hands and paced up and down. Belle would give Linda a shot so she'd sleep instead of lying there in the grip of fear. That was all a GP could do in a case like this. "What?" he asked Rivera.

"I said"—Rivera smiled gently—"she is a saint."

"She sure does a good job of covering it up," Stubbs said.

"All that gruffness hides a very tender heart."

Belle Hesseltine came in from the hall and gave Rivera a sharp look. "Don't talk nonsense." She laid her kit on the sideboard. "Go sit with her." He went, and the old woman came into the circle of light at the table. "What kind of help?" she asked Bohannon, and he jumped to show her the papers. She sat down, put on glasses, and pored over them, pushing them this way and that, briskly, impatiently. Stubbs brought mugs to the table. The clunk of his boot heels was the only sound in the silence. Time passed. Bohannon stood behind her chair, peering at the papers. Stubbs brought the coffeepot and filled the mugs and went back to the stove. More time passed. Then Belle Hesseltine pushed the papers away from her with a bark of derision and took off her glasses. "Rubbish," she said. "Ridiculous."

"My bet is Reva Dahlthorp doesn't think so," Bohannon said.

"That bulldog who runs the nursing home?" Belle Hesseltine said. "What would she know? Has she seen these?"

"No, but I judge she wants to pretty badly," Bohannon said. "Or maybe it's not her." He told the story as quickly and simply as he could, bringing in Prettyman and Wardour. "Whichever one it is, they've got Genevieve." He explained that part. "And they're threatening to kill her."

"And that was where you were off to when I arrived?" Belle Hesseltine peered up at him. "Seriously? What for?"

"To save her life."

"Pshaw, they'd never kill her. What would that get them?" She rose a little stiffly from her chair. She was past seventy, and while she wanted to move like a girl, her joints sometimes said no to that. "It's all bluff. Sit tight. You've got the papers. If they want them, they'll have to come get them, won't they? What happened to your common sense?"

"I'm worried about Linda," he said.

She laid a kindly hand on his arm and gave him a rare smile. "Of course you are. And I'm truly sorry." She went to the sideboard for her kit. "You give some more thought to electroshock treatment. It's not the medieval torture it used to be. I think it's the only answer, Hack." She headed for the door. "You want me to wait till Manfredi comes?"

"No need." Bohannon went and pulled the door open for her. She stepped outside, turned back.

"Gordon Olcott was a fool or a knave or both," she said. "Those patients recovered on their own. That formula of his certainly didn't cure them. It's nothing but snake oil, Hack. He was setting the world up to be made a fool of. Again." She went off along the porch, a stalwart, straight-backed figure, dependable as morning, right as rain. Bohannon called thanks after her and closed the door.

Carlo Manfredi had come and gone. The mental home he operated, one of the finest in the state according to all the checks Bohannon had made, was over the mountains in Atascadero, an old Victorian mansion with jigsaw-work verandahs away from the world in foothills with green lawns and flower beds. Now Linda was on her way back there, asleep in the rear of a big old Cadillac ambulance that ran smoothly and quietly through the darkness outside and her own inner darkness. Hack sat at the kitchen table, coffee grown cold in front of him. He stared at nothing. The phone jarred him out of his bleak reverie. He scraped the chair back, pushed to his feet, knocking down the rifle that he'd leaned against the table. He didn't bother to pick it up. He picked up the telephone.

"It's Teresa," T. Hodges said. "You might want to come down here. Vern drove past that phone again that you asked him about. This time a car was parked there."

"A gray Japanese hatchback," Bohannon said.

"Right. And a stout woman was pushing an older woman toward the phone. He thought she had a gun in her hand, and she did. Reva Dahlthorp. We have her here now."

"Genevieve all right?" Bohannon asked.

"She gave her deposition," T. Hodges said, "and then I drove her to her motel. The poor thing's exhausted. But she wanted me to apologize to you and Linda for all the trouble she's caused."

"Hell, it wasn't her," Bohannon said, "it was Dahlthorp. What's she got to say for herself?"

"Not a word. She phoned her lawyer, and that's that. What's it all about, Hack? Why did she kidnap Genevieve?"

"You mean Genevieve didn't tell you?"

"She doesn't know," T. Hodges said. "For the same reason Dahlthorp turned that attic upside down, I guess, for the same reason she snatched Genevieve's purse. What was it?"

Bohannon told her. "Old Nettie must have rattled on to her about her wonderful doctor son's secret cure for all the world's ailments. Dahlthorp looked after her personally in her last days. And she was fierce about keeping anybody else from talking to the old lady."

"Hack," T. Hodges said strictly, "you have to come down here and put all that on record, you know."

"Tomorrow," Bohannon said. "Good night."

He hung up the phone and limped out to tell Stubbs and Rivera, where they'd been on post in the shadows, that the danger was past. Stubbs could go to bed in his room in the stable building, Rivera could get back up to the seminary. Bohannon returned to the kitchen. He got the whiskey bottle from the sideboard, a glass from a cupboard, and sat at the table again to drink and brood. He had to numb his mind. His body ached with weariness, but he wouldn't sleep tonight. Not sober. He didn't care what Belle Hesseltine said—he was scared of those damned electroshock treatments. Manfredi had described them to him fair and square. And Bohannon couldn't see putting Linda through that. And yet he wanted her back as she used to be. He ached for that. He'd ached for it for years now. If only—

A soft step crunched the gravel outside. He squinted at the window. He listened, holding his breath. Nothing. Slowly, slowly, heart thudding, he bent to pick up the Winchester from the floor. And heels banged the porch boards, the screen door squeaked, the wooden door burst open. A man stood there, holding a revolver. A stocky, gray-haired, red-faced man in a rumpled business suit, the knot of his tie crooked.

"Don't pick up the gun," he said. "Don't make trouble for yourself. I only want what's rightfully mine." He nodded at the stack of big brown envelopes on the table. With surprising quickness he came to the table, placed his foot on the Winchester, picked up the envelopes, tucked them under his arm. He jerked the revolver. "Get up and back away. Hands up. That's right. No, no. Keep on backing. Thank you." He stooped and picked up the Winchester. "All right. I'm going now. But you just stand there for a while." He backed toward the door. Bohannon made to move. The revolver went off. The bullet plowed into the boards between Bohannon's boots. "Do as I say. I may go straight off. Or I may wait outside to see if you can follow orders. If you can't, I'll shoot you." And he was gone.

Bohannon listened as Wardour's shoes crunched quickly away along the gravel. He went to the door and cautiously put his head out. Out in the far dark the revolver cracked and a bullet sang past Bohannon's head. He drew back inside. A car engine revved to life, tires squealed on tarmac. Bohannon ran along the porch, across the gravel to the truck. In the stable, the horses moved restlessly, nickered. Stubbs in a nightshirt came out of his room. He shouted something, but Bohannon couldn't hear it over the clatter of the engine. He backed the truck in a rough arc, scattering gravel. He shouted to Stubbs as he passed, "Look after the horses."

The pickup jounced into the road. He'd forgotten to turn on the headlights, and he damn near collided with a car rushing past the white entry gates of the stable and on down the canyon—a gray hatchback. He switched on his lights and they showed him the license number of the little car. It was Prettyman's. What the hell was going on? He jerked the microphone from its hook under the battered dash and called for help from the sheriff station. His foot was down hard on the gas pedal but this was a narrow, crooked road with steep drops and no guard rails. He put the microphone back quickly. He needed both hands on the shivering wheel. He skidded at a sharp turn, braked hard, and stalled. Damn. He got the motor going again, but he'd lost the cars ahead. Then he got a glimpse of headlights sweeping rocks and scrub, jammed the pickup into gear, raced after them. Too fast. At the next bad bend, the GM skidded off the road and slammed sideways into an oak. He tried to get going again, but the truck only stood with its engine roaring. He knew what was wrong. A broken axle.

He clambered down and was cussing the truck out when sounds came from down the canyon—crunching brush, crumpling, squealing metal, heavy slams, shattering glass. He clawed up the bluff above the oak and looked. In the pitch dark, fire suddenly flared up. He heard the crackling, though he could only see the glow. He slid on his butt down to the pickup, grabbed the fire extinguisher, and ran down the road with it. It seemed a long way. He was staggering and breathing hard when he came up to Prettyman standing beside his car, staring down into a deep ravine where Wardour's car lay burning, wheels in the air. The firelight playing on his face, Prettyman glanced at Bohannon.

"That won't be any use," he said.

"Afraid you're right," Bohannon said.

"Don't worry. Wardour got thrown clear. I saw it, I'm glad you showed up. I couldn't drag him out of there. Not with my bad back. Not alone."

"Where do we look?" Bohannon said.

"Come on." Prettyman started carefully down the slope, his shoes breaking twigs, dislodging rocks. "I began looking for him soon as you left my place. I located him just as he was starting up here. Whoa!" Prettyman's foot slipped, he sat down. "I hope I don't end up in a hospital after this."

"Take it easy," Bohannon said.

They found William Wardour sitting on a rock, clutching what was plainly a broken arm. His suit was torn, his face scraped and bleeding, his hair full of grass and twigs. He stared at the burning car. Bohannon spoke his name, and he looked up miserably. "My father's wonderful formula. He told my mother it was going to end sickness forever. Even cancer. I waited all these years to get my hands on it. Think of the money. Now look."

"Forget it," Bohannon said. "He lied to your mother. It was nothing but kickapoo juice."

And from down the canyon came the wail of sirens.

The Owl in
the Oak

Alice Donovan was a small woman, past forty but brisk, with an open way about her, a smile and a perky word for just about everybody. She called her shop Ye Olde Oak Tree for the very good reason that an old oak sheltered it. Like a good many shops in Madrone, hers had been converted from a spindly frame dwelling with jigsaw-work porches and bay windows. Most of these places sported fresh paint nowadays. Ye Olde Oak Tree was green with yellow trim.

The last time Hack Bohannon had noticed, Alice sold cheap china and pewter knickknacks, T-shirts and souvenir scarves, picture postcards, sunglasses, snapshot film, chewing gum, cigarettes—and cookies, when she felt like baking. She kept antiques that needed work. Bohannon recollected a treadle sewing machine in the front yard, an old wooden Maytag with hand-cranked wringers. A wagon wheel had leaned against the trunk of the oak. Bad oil paintings slumped on the porch, seascapes mostly—the ocean was over yonder, on the far side of the highway.

All this was gone now. Neat beds of pansies and petunias lay to either side of the footpath. Bohannon's boot heels knocked across an empty porch. And when he opened the door and stepped inside, he didn't recognize the place. New paint, wallpaper, carpet on the floor. The antique rockers, highboys, commodes were sleekly refinished. Not a postcard rack remained, no T-shirts, visor hats, suntan lotion. Good Mexican terra-cotta pots stood on shelves. Fine baskets occupied corners. Soft serapes in natural wool colors hung against the walls. On velvet in glass cases lay bracelets, necklaces, rings in hand-wrought silver set with turquoise and jade.

The shop took up the two front rooms of the little house—parlor, sitting room. He stepped behind a counter and opened an inner door. Built-in diamond-paned sideboards said this had been a dining room. Magazines, books, cassettes, a camera, and boxes of film crowded them now. The room had only space enough for two wing chairs, a coffee table, a television set—and these were all it held. He pushed a swinging door and was in the kitchen. A deputy had used a black Magic Marker on the pale vinyl tile of the floor to outline where and how Alice Donovan's small body had lain when her hulking son Howard had found it last night. Next to a glass of white wine on a counter, slices of apple and a wedge of yellow cheese lay on a saucer, a paring knife in the sink.

The back door stood open, and he frowned at that. Gerard ought to have posted an officer here. Bohannon squinted at the door and the frame. A deadbolt had been broken. Someone had wanted badly to get in. Early this morning, as soon as news of the murder got on the radio. A size-twelve shoe had forced the door, a shoe muddy from the dew in the brush out back. He scowled around him. Had bigfoot found what Bohannon was here to look for? That would be a hell of a note.

Morning sunlight came cheerfully through a window over the sink and slanted onto the place where Alice Donovan had died. The patch of dried blood there was the size of a dinner plate. Someone had smashed her skull in, unhooked a cast-iron skillet from its place in a row of pans over the stove and hit her from behind. Lieutenant Gerard of the Madrone sheriff's office figured big, shambling Howard had done it. Howard was sitting in a cell. He claimed he had been on the beach, alone all evening, thinking. He had killed eight cans of beer. The empties were there, bobbing in the surf among the rocks to prove it, if anyone cared to check.

"And many more besides," Gerard grunted, "I have no doubt. Christ, people love to make the world ugly, don't they?" He wadded the last bite of a cruller into his mouth and washed it down with coffee from a chipped mug. "No, Howard and Alice had been on a collision course since he was born. She babied him through years one to thirteen, then made him the man in her life, right? Except he could never do what he wanted, only what she wanted."

"You could say"—Bohannon tilted back in a straight oak chair—"he went direct from the nursing bottle to the whiskey bottle."

Howard had spent times away from Madrone in hospitals that promise to cure addictive personalities and sometimes succeed—though not with Howard. He wasn't much more than twenty, but no peace officer who'd ever had to deal with him, Bohannon not excepted, figured him for less than a dangerous drunk for life—or at least for as long as he lasted. He was quite a driver when he drank. He had totaled two cars of his mother's, and others that had belonged to former friends.

"His buddies don't want him around," Bohannon said.

"Except Beau Larkin," Gerard said. "Worse than Howard. Beau'd be in Folsom if his dad wasn't a San Luis cop."

"Howard never got violent with Alice. Not once."

"There's always a first time." Gerard crumpled the white paper sack the cruller had come in and dropped it into a wastebasket. "Nothing was stolen, Hack. Whoever did it didn't have to force entry. No, Howard came home drunk, and they had another argument—their last one."

"Fred May doesn't think so," Bohannon said.

"Right. And that's why you're here." Gerard pawed the files, photographs, reports on his desk and found cigarettes. He lit one and looked at Bohannon through the smoke. "Fred wants you to find evidence that somebody else killed Alice Donovan."

He gave a thin smile. "You do as much police work as you used to when you were on the payroll here, Hack. Why don't you just come back, and stop being so stubborn?"

Bohannon had been a deputy for fourteen years; then it had gone sour for him. He would never come back to work here. He hated the very sounds and smells of the place, the desks, files, jangling phones, even the lighting. He and Gerard had been partners, friends. They weren't enemies now, but they'd never be the same again.

"Give me the keys," Bohannon said. "I'll go see if Fred's got a case or not."

When Bohannon passed May's office, May came waddling out of it and walked beside him down the hallway. May, on the staff of the county attorney, was a public defender when the need arose. He was no paper shuffler but a bright lawyer with a belief in justice nothing could shake—certainly not offers of money. He would have been better paid almost anyplace else. Luckily, his wife and kids were as decent as he was. If a battered VW bug was wheels enough for him, if he could get through the days in sweatshirts, cheap jeans, and worn-out tennis shoes, so could they, and cheerfully. Bohannon pushed open the side door of the substation, and the fat man followed him out to the parking lot, where patrol cars stood collecting leaves and pods from the towering eucalypts that hedged the tarmac.

May said, "You know what bothers me? Not that nothing was stolen. What bothers me is that Alice Donovan had anything worth stealing. Where did she get the money to upgrade the place so suddenly?"

"Why not from the bank?" Bohannon had lately wrecked his faithful old GM pickup, and the one parked out here now was new, shiny, apple-green. He pulled open the door and climbed up into it. It didn't smell of alfalfa and dried manure yet. It still smelled new. He kept thinking it didn't belong to him. "She owned the property, didn't she? Why didn't she take out a loan on it?"

"I don't know"—May's moon face winced up at him—"but

she didn't. Not in this area. We checked it out. See what you can find, Hack. There's an answer someplace."

"She didn't tell Howard?" Bohannon slammed the door of the pickup and slid the key into the ignition. "Or is he too hung over to talk?"

"He's not hung over, but she said it was a secret. She teased him, like he was five years old: 'I've got a secret, I won't tell—' "

"Don't sing, Fred," Bohannon said.

"Sorry about that. But he did say something interesting. Said he saw her hide something. If it was money, Howard wanted it. For booze, right? When he thought it was safe, he dug it out, but she caught him before he could open it."

"So he doesn't know if it was money or what." Bohannon started the truck. Over the smooth hum of the engine May said, "A cardboard box with rubber bands around it. He looked for it again, every chance he got, but he never found it."

"Maybe I'll have better luck." Bohannon released the hand brake. "I won't have to worry about Alice walking in on me, will I?" He lifted a hand and drove off.

Now, in the silent kitchen, he got down on hands and knees to probe low cupboards that smelled of soap powder. He climbed a flimsy aluminum step stool to grope on high shelves among cobwebby cut glass, cracked plates, forgotten gift boxes of fancy teas. In a shadowy hallway he unloaded sheets, pillowcases, towels from a linen closet. Nothing. He got the step stool and poked his head through a ceiling trapdoor. Nothing but rafters, dust, and heat.

Alice Donovan's bedroom was neat and smelled faintly of sandalwood perfume. He found nothing that didn't belong there. She wouldn't hide whatever it was in Howard's room, but he searched that anyway. Empty pint vodka bottles rattled among the cleated shoes on the closet floor. The closet smelled of the sweaty jeans, shirts, jackets that hung there. On the shelf lay shoulder pads, helmets, a catcher's mitt, and a stack of dog-eared magazines with photos of naked young women. The bed was unmade. In the dust balls under it lay empty beer cans and crumpled potato chip bags.

The bedside stand held a lamp and a digital clock with red numerals that read 12:00. Plainly, Howard hadn't bothered setting it again after the last power outage. Maybe time, along with everything else but his thirst, had ceased to have meaning for Howard. Bohannon opened a drawer in the table. Candy bar wrappers, scratched California lottery tickets, rubber bands, a broken pencil. And photographs. Half a dozen. Of a red-haired young woman who looked tall. Taken someplace among boats—Morro Bay? She wore tight jeans, a striped tank top, sunglasses that didn't hide her exceptional good looks. He tucked the photos into a shirt pocket and went to check out the bathroom.

It was shiny clean, and Alice Donovan had not hidden anything there. Back in the kitchen, he opened the refrigerator. He'd never seen so many cans of beer outside a market. He took one, figuring Howard wouldn't mind, since Bohannon was trying to save his sizable hide. A noise came from the shop. He must have left the door unlocked. He set down the beer can and jogged for the front rooms. A large, expensively dressed woman was peering into one of the glass cases. She turned and stared at him in surprise. He understood. In his Levis, cowboy boots, Stetson, he plainly was no dealer in jewelry and antiques.

"Who—who are you?" A thick envelope was in her hand. She poked it hastily into a large handbag. "What are you doing here?"

"Investigator for the county attorney," he said. "Bohannon is my name. What's yours?"

"Where's Mrs. Donovan?" She came toward him, peering past his shoulder through the open door into the living quarters. She called out, "Alice? It's Erica Weems." She looked at Bohannon. "We had an appointment." She read a tiny jeweled watch on a wrist strong enough to control an eight-horse hitch. "For twelve noon." She blinked. "Investigator?"

"Mrs. Donovan met with an accident," Bohannon said.

Erica Weems went very still. Fashion wasn't doing her kind any favors. The exaggerated shoulders of the moment made her look like a linebacker in drag. Her tongue touched her lips. He couldn't read the look in her eyes. "Is she—all right? An automobile accident, you mean?"

Bohannon shook his head. "Assault. She's dead."

"My God." The woman's knees gave. Bohannon stepped out from behind the counter to catch her arm, but she didn't want that. She sat down, breathing hard, clutching the purse tight against her. She managed a pale, apologetic smile. "Excuse me. I'll just sit here a moment, if I may. It's such a shock."

"Get you anything?" he asked. "Water? Brandy?"

Eyes closed, she shook her head. "Assault. How dreadful." She opened her eyes. "She was so tiny."

"Were you a friend?" Bohannon said.

"Friend?" Her brief laugh had no humor in it. "No. Just a —customer." Her gaze caressed the jewelry, pottery, weaving. "She had such lovely things, didn't she?"

"You used her first name," Bohannon said. "If you were a friend, I thought maybe you could help me here."

Her look was guarded. "Help you how? With what?"

He shrugged. "If you talked together, maybe she said something—was she frightened of anything, anyone?"

Erica Weems snorted. "Have you met her son?"

Bohannon grinned. "He once lifted me up over his head and threw me into the ocean. He and his high school friends got a little rowdy that night. Howard's a big, strong boy."

"I don't know how she could bear having him here."

"He's been locked up for the murder," Bohannon said. "I'm supposed to find evidence he didn't do it."

Erica Weems gave a wry laugh. "I wish you luck," she said, and got off the chair, and walked out. Bohannon wanted to ask her what was in that envelope she'd stuffed so hurriedly into her handbag. But it would be smarter to wait. He watched her settle into a Mercedes that looked as if it got washed and waxed every day. He watched it roll off down the dusty trail, then went back to the kitchen to finish off his beer and nail shut the back door.

He found the box twenty minutes later, in a spring-operated compartment hidden behind a beautifully mitered drawer in a General Grant lowboy with a marble top. He sat on the fresh crimson velvet of a carved walnut chair, twanged the rubber bands from around the box, and lifted the lid. A sour smell came out. Inside lay a stack of small envelopes, note-size, fastened by another rubber band. When he lifted them out, he saw a little packet of olive-drab velvet, the same fabric that lined Alice Donovan's glass display cases.

He unfolded the velvet from around a piece of Navajo jewelry, a buckle. Not new like the stuff the Donovan woman was selling. Old. The stone was brown, not blue or green, and the heft of the piece, its timeworn smoothness, told him it was special. He rewrapped it and tucked it into his shirt pocket with the snapshots of the red-haired girl. Then he snapped the rubber band off the envelopes and shuffled through them. They were stained and gritty to the touch.

All were addressed in ballpoint pen to an Estella Hernandez at a post office box in Guadalupe. There was no return address. He pulled a letter out of its envelope. It was signed only G. He read it and blinked. G seemed pretty worked up. He folded that letter and put it back in its envelope and read the others, one by one. G evidently thought he was in love. Starlight and birdsongs and the moon shining on a midnight ocean got into the letters, but so did steamy sexual stuff. One of the letters, the first one, was signed Galen. The postmarks were all Madrone. He rubber-banded the envelopes, stuffed them into a pocket of his Levi jacket, put the empty box back into the lowboy, closed the drawer, and left Alice Donovan's silent shop, locking the door behind him.

Halfway down the path, he paused to squint up at the oak. Crows were making a racket there, flapping around, diving at something hidden in the leafage. It was an owl, a big Western horned owl. He hunched on a branch, and looked like he meant to stay there, like it was his tree, and the crows could do their damnedest but he wasn't leaving. He glared up at them with round yellow eyes and clacked his beak at them from time to time, and now and then spread his wings and bounced up and down as if on springs. Then he'd crouch again, screwing his head around to face them, this way, that way, no matter from what angle they came at him. Bohannon wished him luck and climbed into his new pickup.

Deputy T. Hodges was seated at a little square table on the screened porch of a luncheonette in Madrone. The tabletop was Formica in a red gingham pattern. A red paper napkin lay crumped beside T. Hodges' plate. The remains of a hamburger and a scattering of french fries lay on the plate. She was nursing what Bohannon guessed was cold coffee. When he banged in at the screen door, her shiny dark eyes lit up for a second in a smile. By the time he pulled the empty chair out at her table, she was frowning. She read her watch.

"I've only got ten minutes left," she said.

"Sorry." He sat down. "I was looking for something and I wasn't too quick about finding it. You haven't had dessert. Shall we eat peach pie together?"

A fat girl in a sweatshirt stenciled RAIDERS came to the table and took a pencil from behind her ear. "Mr. Bohannon. Hi. How's my pal Geranium?"

Geranium was a broad-backed, placid old buckskin mare who never put a big hoof wrong, and Cassie felt safe on her when she came up to the stables with one of her assorted boyfriends to ride the canyon trails on Mondays, when the café was closed.

"She missed you the other day," Bohannon said.

"I went swimming." She made a face. "Tony said we were going sailing in his boat, but he kept tipping it over. What will you have?"

"Peach pie for both of us," Bohannon said. "And Deputy Hodges needs a refill, and I'll have coffee, too, please."

"You got it," Cassie said, took T. Hodges' plate, and padded away.

"Looking for what?" T. Hodges said.

He told her. Then he laid the snapshots in front of her. "Ever see that girl before?"

"Howard had these?" Marveling, she shuffled them. "Yes, it's Andrea Norse." She gave an exaggerated sigh of envy and laid the photos down. "Stunning."

"College girl?" he said.

"She's past thirty, Hack, believe it or not. No, she's a psychological counselor for the county, family relations, that kind of thing. I suppose"—she touched the photos, lining them up —"that was how Howard met her, right?"

"Sounds logical." Bohannon scooped up the pictures and put them away. "Only what was she doing on a date with him? Letting him take her picture?"

"Maybe he didn't," she said. "Why not ask her?"

"I will." Bohannon laid the little packet of velvet on the table and unfolded it. "What does this suggest to you?"

T. Hodges' eyes opened wide. She picked up the Navajo piece and studied it. "Stolen," she said.

"You're sure?"

She nodded. "From a private collection of old Indian jewelry in San Luis. The Kanter collection. By housebreakers six months ago. Every piece had been photographed, of course, for insurance company records. The San Luis police sent out fliers illustrated with the photos. I can dig ours out for you if you want."

"Valuable, then," Bohannon said. Cassie came with the coffeepot and two slices of pie. She filled their mugs and admired the Navajo piece. "That's pretty." She looked enviously at T. Hodges. "He giving you that? What is it—your birthday or something?"

"It's stolen," T. Hodges said. "He's under arrest."

"I'll phone the TV news," Cassie said, and went away.

"In the neighborhood of a hundred thousand dollars." T. Hodges wrapped the piece up again. "For the whole collection, I mean." She held the little packet out, and Bohannon put it back into his shirt pocket. She cut into her pie. "What was Alice Donovan doing with something so valuable?"

"Why wasn't she the thief?" Bohannon said.

"Because the thief is in jail and the collection is back with the Kanters, all but this piece, which the thief insists he didn't sell. He didn't have time."

Bohannon ate pie, drank coffee, and thought. "Some kind of insurance scam on the part of the owners?"

"I think Mr. Kanter owns most of San Luis."

"Do you know exactly when Alice upgraded that shop?"

"About a year ago," T. Hodges said. "Mmm. This pie is heavenly."

"About a year ago a local man named Galen had an affair with a Guadalupe woman called Estella Hernandez."

"Ah—those letters you mentioned?"

"You know any man named Galen in Madrone?" Bohannon lit a cigarette and drank coffee. "It's not a common name."

"No Galens," she said. "You'll have to ask Estella Hernandez, won't you?"

"If I can find her. From the letters, I take it she lived in a trailer, mobile home. She could be long gone by now." He gave his head a shake. "What do you think? Was Alice Donovan into extortion? Freddy May says she didn't borrow the money to fix up the business. She couldn't have saved anything from the operation the way it was, nickels and dimes. And Howard must have cost a lot, smashing cars and having to be dried out in hospitals."

"So she blackmailed this Galen?" T. Hodges polished off her pie. "And Galen finally got fed up and stepped into the kitchen last night and bashed her head in with a skillet? Then why didn't he take the letters away with him?"

"I told you—they were hidden. No time to look for them.

Howard got home very soon after she was killed. The killer would have had to hightail it not to be caught." Bohannon finished his coffee, took a long last drag from the cigarette, put it out. "Maybe it was Galen who came back early this morning and kicked in the back door, hoping to find the letters."

"And never found them," T. Hodges said.

"We better go." Bohannon got to his feet, slid bills from a worn wallet, laid them on the table for Cassie. He held open the screen door for T. Hodges. At the foot of the steps, on the crooked little trail, she read her watch again and looked woebegone.

"I'm really late," she said.

"I'll drive you back," he said.

He wanted to report to Fred May, but May was in court. So Bohannon drove down through the dunes, headed for Guadalupe. He didn't get there. He found a trailer park in a swale on the land side of the beach highway. The office had a temporary look to it, plywood and studs, but it had been there awhile—the wood had darkened from rain, sun, wind, and salt spray. It had warped, too. When someone called, "Come in," from behind the door, he had to shoulder the door to get it open. It scraped the floor. The plywood counter had little bonsai trees on it, and a tiny Japanese woman in a wash-faded housedress was snipping at the branches of the trees, craftily, keeping them stunted, and perfect. Her face was like a withered apple. She smiled at him with crooked brown teeth and gave a little bow.

Bohannon touched his hat brim. "One of your tenants an Estella Hernandez?"

Her answer made him think of an owner's manual he'd got with a stereo he and Linda had bought some years back. It was in English, all right, but neither of them had been able to understand it. But the little lady was used to this, it looked like. She laughed at herself, came from behind the counter, took his elbow, led him back outside, and pointed out the Hernandez trailer to him.

It was like the rest of them there, halfhearted efforts at looking like tract houses. Like the rest, it had been some time since it had rolled down any highway on wheels. A tin awning held up by spindly pipes sheltered the side of the place. A skinny brown boy of maybe ten sat on the doorstep with a scuba diver's mask in his hand. When he heard the crunch of gravel under Bohannon's boots, he looked at him, got off the steps, and walked away, glum resignation in the slump of his shoulders, the way he scuffed the ground. Bohannon pulled open a flimsy screen and knocked on the door.

From inside, a woman's voice called to him in Spanish.

"It's Galen," he said. "Open up, Estella."

She opened the door, a dark, slim young woman, heavy breasts in a flower-print halter, a very tight pair of jeans, bare feet with crimson toenails. She blinked long, furry black lashes at him, and gave a short, mocking laugh. "One thing I do know is voices," she said. "Galen has a high voice." She tilted her head and smiled while her glance ran up and down him. "If you sang, you would sing bass." She frowned, puzzled. "Did Galen send you?" She glanced up at the sun. "It is early in the day."

"Galen didn't send me," he said, and took out his wallet. "And I'm not a client." He showed her his license. "I'm with the county attorney. I need to find Galen."

"What for?" She waved a mocking hand at the wallet. "You don't mean to tell me Galen has committed a crime." She laughed. "He would not have the courage."

"What's his last name, Estella? Where does he live?"

"How do you know about him and me?"

Bohannon showed her the letters.

"I threw those in the garbage," she said.

"That's what they smell like," Bohannon said.

She made a bitter face. "That is what they are."

"You know Galen wouldn't have sent me or any other man here. He was in love with you."

"He is a crazy fool. He nearly got both of us killed with his stupid jealousy."

"He didn't like your line of work?" Bohannon said.

She snorted. "A romantic teenager of fifty years of age. A married man. With a grandchild."

"His last name, please, Estella?"

She narrowed her eyes. "What is it worth to the county attorney's office?"

"Worth not getting busted for prostitution," Bohannon told her, "and for keeping a child on unfit premises."

She sighed grimly. "Why did I think you would be different? It don't matter how good-looking, a cop is a cop. His name is Worthy. Isn't that a joke?"

"And what's his line of work?" Bohannon said.

"He is a dentist." Her laugh was dry. "Galen, the first Galen in history, you know, was a famous Greek physician. He told me this. So his parents wanted him to be a doctor, but he failed medical school. You've got to have brains to be a doctor."

G. B. Worthy's offices were on the second floor of a brick business building in Madrone that didn't show its brick to the street anymore. The front had been dressed in pecky cedar boards. The notion was to make the town look like the Wild West of 1880. Bohannon didn't much like that. The waiting room had bland framed prints on the walls, a pair of couches, a coffee table, a rack of magazines, a green tank of lazily swimming tropical fish. With a knuckle he touched the opaque glass of a service window. The woman who slid the glass back he pegged as Mrs. Worthy. She was stout, middle-aged, and fixed her hair around her head in bulky braids, yellow hair tinged with gray. She smiled with stunning teeth. "Have you an appointment?"

"I need some help from the doctor," Bohannon said, and

showed her his license. "It's a law enforcement matter. It shouldn't take long."

She nodded knowingly, as if law enforcement matters were daily occurrences around there, as if the doctor were consulted by peace officers routinely, said, "One moment, please," closed the sliding glass. Voices murmured, then an inner door opened and a good-looking man, trim, slim, mustached, smiled and held out a hand. He said, "Whose dental charts do you want to see, Mr. Bohannon?"

Bohannon took the hand, gave Galen Worthy a conspiratorial look, and drew him out into the waiting room. He said softly, "Tell her we're going for coffee."

Worthy frowned and pulled his hand away. "What for? I don't understand. A police matter, my wife said."

Bohannon murmured, "The death of Alice Donovan. You want to discuss that here?"

"I—I don't know what you're talking about." Worthy's Adam's apple pumped. He turned a bad color. "Alice who?"

Bohannon pulled the smelly letters from his pocket and held them out so the dentist could get a good look. "Donovan. These were in her possession. You wrote them. Or so Estella Hernandez says."

The glass panel slid open. Mrs. Worthy said, "Galen, is everything all right?" She eyed Bohannon dubiously.

Her husband gave her a nervous smile. "It's all right, dear. But I have to go out for a few minutes."

"I won't keep him long," Bohannon told her.

They got into the pickup and Bohannon headed out of town, which didn't mean far in a little place like Madrone. They parked on a dusty foothill road.

Worthy had been silent. Now he burst out, "There are supposed to be two kinds of luck. Why do I always have the bad kind?"

"They say we make our own." Bohannon lit a cigarette.

"You'll kill yourself with those," Worthy snapped at him. "Worse than that, you'll kill those around you."

"I won't, but those letters could," Bohannon said. "How did the Donovan woman get hold of them, anyway?"

Worthy made a sour noise meant for a laugh. "Found them. You know how people dump their trash up in the canyons? Just drive along to a lonely spot and heave it out off the edge of the road. Disgusting."

"Go on," Bohannon said.

Worthy rolled down the window and waved a hand in front of his face to fend off the smoke. "Well, Alice had sent Howard on some errand, and he was hours late getting back. It was going to be dark soon. Knowing him, she figured he'd gotten drunk and passed out somewhere. So she borrowed a neighbor's car and went to find him. He'd driven off the road down a steep embankment. The car had come to rest in a huge pile of plastic trash bags."

"From Estella's trailer camp, right?" Bohannon said.

Worthy's mouth twitched. "And bags had split open and spilled, hadn't they? And here were my letters strewn around for all the world to read. And the rest you know, don't you? How my money smartened up that shop for her?"

"To save your marriage?" Bohannon patted the letters in his side pocket. "I thought you loved Estella."

"Doris—Mrs. Worthy—put me through dental school after my own family gave up on me. I owe her everything."

"And it doesn't matter if you're a good dentist or not," Bohannon said, "she keeps you in style, right?"

"I didn't kill Alice Donovan," Worthy said.

"What size shoe do you wear, doctor?" Bohannon said.

Worthy blinked. "What kind of question is that?"

"Somebody heard on the early morning news that Alice was dead and hustled over to her shop and kicked in the back door with a size-twelve shoe. Why wasn't it you, trying to get hold of these letters ahead of the sheriff?"

"It wasn't me." Worthy shook his head hard. "I drove straight to the office. You found the letters, not me."

"I didn't say you found them, only looked for them."

"I wasn't anywhere near there. I didn't know she was dead until you told me. We don't put the TV on in the mornings. Ask Doris."

Bohannon looked at him with his eyebrows raised.

"No. I don't mean that. She mustn't know."

"You and she go to work in the same car?" Bohannon said.

"She goes first to get things ready. I follow later."

"So you can't prove you didn't detour past Alice's."

Worthy said stubbornly, "And you can't prove I did." He read his watch. "I have to get back. I have appointments."

"What about last night?" Bohannon crushed out his cigarette in the dashboard ashtray and pushed the little metal drawer shut. "Around midnight. You weren't at Alice's then, either?"

"I was in bed, asleep."

Bohannon twisted the key in the ignition and the new engine hummed to life. He couldn't get used to its quiet after the clatter of his old truck. It took him by surprise every time. Sometimes he didn't know the damned thing had started at all. He glanced at the dentist.

"You know, if you were there, either last night or this morning, chances are somebody saw you. Alice's place isn't the only one on that road. There are neighbors. It's not a dead end. It's on the way. People drive it. So if you'd like to change your story before it begins to fall apart, now is the time to do it."

Worthy stared straight ahead through the clean windshield. "It isn't a story," he said, "it's the truth."

"Then you've got nothing to be tense about." Bohannon reached over and touched the tight fist on the dentist's knee. Worthy jerked the hand away as if from an electric shock. "Relax," Bohannon said. "If anybody tells your wife, it won't be me."

"Give me back those letters," Worthy pleaded.

"Later," Bohannon said.

• •

"What you have to know," he told Fred May, "is that somebody big got there before me this morning and broke the lock on the back door."

"And it wasn't Howard," the fat man said, smiling. "Good work, Hack. Who was it?" He touched the stained envelopes on his desk. "The dentist?"

"His feet are too small." Bohannon stared out the window, smoking, a can of beer in his hand. "And he claims he wasn't there. If he was, he didn't find the letters."

"It couldn't have been the Weems woman?" Fred May rocked back in his oak swivel chair and the spring twanged. "You say she's big."

"She still doesn't wear size-twelve shoes." Bohannon took a swallow of beer, watched smoke from his cigarette drift out the window into the warm, late-afternoon air. "And I don't think she knew Alice Donovan was dead."

"You really think she came to make a payment to her?" He poked with a fat finger at the Navajo buckle that lay on its ragged little square of velvet among the typed, blue-papered briefs and law books on the desk. "To keep Alice from revealing she was in possession of stolen property?"

Bohannon frowned and shook his head. "It doesn't make sense, Fred." He flicked the spent cigarette out the window into a flower bed and dropped onto an oak chair. "Why pay a blackmailer when you could easily explain to the San Luis police that you'd bought it innocently? It would be cheaper to take the loss on what she'd paid for it than to keep shelling out to Alice for the rest of her life."

"Then there's something Alice had around the place you didn't find." May drank diet soda from a can. "Or did the early riser who kicked in the door find it?"

"There wasn't any sign anybody had done any searching for anything." Bohannon finished his beer and tossed the empty can into the brown metal wastebasket beside May's desk, and made a face. "If bigfoot even came inside, he found what he wanted right there in the kitchen, or what he thought was there wasn't."

"What would it be?" May's forehead wrinkled.

"When I find him, I'll ask him." With a sigh, Bohannon got to his feet. It had been a long day. He was tired. "Meantime, I need the key to Alice's cash register."

May said, "Right here," opened a drawer, and took out a little flat key. Bohannon held his hand out, and May put the key into it. "What do you expect to find?"

Bohannon grinned and tossed the key in his hand. "Photographs of a very large middle-aged lady," he said, "doing something she shouldn't."

The house was an expensive one on the beach, stone and beams, and gloomy smoked glass on the road side. From the road where he left the pickup, he looked down on the flat roof of the house, which was covered in rocks white as chalk. He went down sandy stone steps into a cavelike entryway and put his thumb on a bell push. He stood listening to the silky rush and retreat of waves on the beach, and then the door opened. It wasn't the Weems woman. It was a young man, dressed in next to nothing. He was smooth and tan. His lean musculature looked carved. His hair was curly and black and he wore it long. Bohannon wondered on what beach Erica Weems had found him.

Bohannon wasn't a type he'd encountered before. He looked puzzled, but he didn't say anything.

"Mrs. Weems here?" Bohannon gave his name. "We met this morning. Tell her. She'll remember me."

The young man blinked. Something was happening under all that theatrical hair. Maybe he was thinking. At last, with a small shrug, he turned and went down a long room whose far end had a wall of glass that showed the beach and the sea. The sun was lowering and the light on the water was turning flame-colored. The young man stepped outside. Bohannon stepped inside, shut the door behind him, went down the long room.

The young man was back in the open panel of the glass wall in no time.

"What do you want?" he said in a French accent.

"I have something for Mrs. Weems from Alice Donovan's shop." He raised his voice, in case Erica Weems was within earshot. "She'll want to see it."

The young man stepped toward him. "You must telephone and make the appointment." He reached for Bohannon's arm. Bohannon didn't want to knock him down, but he wasn't about to leave. He shook the hand off. The youth tried again, and a voice reached them both. Erica Weems stood in the open glass panel. Her white terry-cloth robe made her look like a polar bear.

"Oh, Mr. Bohannon." Her smile was nervous, and she lied. "I misunderstood. Jean-Marie's accent puzzles me sometimes." She tried for a laugh and missed. She came to them, gently but firmly pried the youth away from Bohannon, and aimed him at an inner doorway. "Dear Jean, be a darling and find us all some bubbly, will you?"

"Beer," Bohannon said, "thanks."

Jean-Marie scowled like a six-year-old, but after a second's pause, he grumbled away, glancing back menacingly at the pair of them. A jealous lover in the authentic Gallic mode, out of a silent movie. Funny.

Erica Weems put a finger to her lips and led Bohannon out onto the deck, across the deck, down to the sand. She took his arm and hustled him along the sand. "You've got the pictures. That's what you found at Alice's shop, isn't it? Those dreadful pictures. Give them to me."

"You were paying Alice to keep quiet about them."

"I'll pay you. The money's in the house. Only give them to me. And the negatives? She said I could have the negatives this time."

"I don't think so," Bohannon said.

Her face fell. She let him go. "What?"

"I don't think she'd give you those." He gestured at the house. "You're well fixed, it appears to me. No, I think she'd bleed you with those pictures forever."

She sighed. "Of course. You're right. Awful woman."

"Where were you at midnight last night?" he said.

"We had a party," she said. "It was very lively. Young people. Music. Jean-Marie is a singer, you know. And a song writer. Guitar. Piano. He has a wonderful future. Everyone says so."

"Good," Bohannon said. "How late did this party run?"

"Until almost sunrise," she said.

"And you stayed until the last guest left?"

She gave him a rueful laugh. "Those were the days, weren't they? No, I was in bed by one-thirty, two. You can ask any of them—and you will, won't you?"

"When you give me the guest list," he said.

"Right away," she said.

Jean-Marie came along the sand, carrying a tray on which glasses glittered. All by his lonesome he turned this stretch of beach into the Côte d'Azur. There should have been a bevy of bikini-clad nymphets in his wake. Bohannon looked at Erica Weems. She was watching the French lad as if she'd never seen anything so delicious in her life—and maybe she hadn't.

"Is it him Alice Donovan was threatening to show those photos to?" The photos had been taken in supermarkets and department stores. Alice must have followed her around for weeks with that camera hidden in a shopping bag. Erica Weems was a shoplifter. Not the first person-who-had-everything Bohannon had run into who couldn't keep from stealing. It was some kind of emotional short circuit. A bid for attention? Maybe once Jean-Marie came along, she'd given it up. "Would he leave you?"

She flushed. "Of course not. No, she'd have shown them to my husband. He'd divorce me. I'd lose everything."

"He doesn't object to Jean-Marie?"

"I'm only helping Jean-Marie with his career."

"Where is Mr. Weems these days?" Bohannon said.

"In Hong Kong. He owns electronics parts firms there. Also in Taiwan and South Korea. He's away much of the time."

"Too bad," Bohannon said.

Jean-Marie arrived with his tray. She beamed at him. "Dear boy," she said, and took a tulip champagne glass from the tray. While the French lad filled it, the Weems woman turned her smile on Bohannon. "I miss Ralph, of course, but I manage to struggle along without him—somehow."

Bohannon took a glass and a bottle of Beck's from the tray. "I see that you do," he said, and poured his beer.

They sat down on the sand. Mrs. Weems rubbed a big terry-cloth shoulder against the boy's naked one. She said, "Mr. Bohannon works for the—uh—county attorney, and for reasons I can't hope to understand, he needs a list of our guests last night. Will you find it, please?"

The boy didn't turn to her. He watched leggy little shore birds getting in their last long-beaked probings of the glassy sand before nightfall. Maybe he was making up a song. He certainly wasn't worried. "*Oui,*" he said.

Bohannon got in and out of his truck often in the next three hours. Each time he was behind the steering wheel again, he unfolded the list Jean-Marie had given him, and at the end the paper was coming apart. He sighed and tucked it away. He was on a twisty road with few street lamps in Settlers Cove, a section of houses hidden among pines on hills beside the sea. Because they were farthest off, he had first checked on the partygoers in Morro Bay and Los Osos. So far as any of them remembered—a skinny girl painter, a fortyish male dancer who wore mascara, a squat bald screenwriter in flowered knee-length surfer shorts—Erica Weems had not only been highly visible in the house and on the beach at her place until the wee hours but had been the life of the party. They all liked good old Erica. Oysters chilled on the half shell, duck pâté, lobster, and all the champagne you could drink. Really, Erica was something else.

And the story had been the same among the sighing night pines of Settlers Cove. He'd heard it here from a reed player with spiky blue hair, from a music video producer with one leg in a cast, from Mitch Russell, the big, bushy-bearded man who ran the little theater in Madrone. No point bothering anyone else. Bohannon started the truck and headed for home, food, a shower, and bed.

When Bohannon stopped the truck at the far end of the long, white, green-trimmed stable building, pulled the parking brake, and killed the engine, George Stubbs came out of his sleeping quarters next to the tack room. He was an ex–rodeo rider, a fat old man now, who hobbled, his bones and joints remembering long-ago breaks and sprains. Bohannon climbed wearily down out of the truck and slammed the door in the night silence. Horses stirred in their dark box stalls behind closed doors and nickered softly. Mountains loomed above the place, dark and shaggy. The air was cool.

Stubbs limped up, looking a little peeved. His thick fingers, with their arthritis-swollen joints, were smudged with charcoal. Likely he'd been drawing in his room. He loved to draw—most commonly horses—and did it well and took pride in it. "Where you been all day and half the night? Couldn't you find a phone?"

"A crisis, was there?" Bohannon started for the house. "Anybody dead?"

Stubbs followed him. "Pretty dead supper in the oven, but I reckon that's my own fault, bothering about you."

"I'm sorry I didn't phone, George. I won't let it happen again." A long, covered plank walk fronted the ranch house. Bohannon went along it to the kitchen, pulled the screen door, walked over to the big stove rearing up in a corner. He pulled open the door to the warming oven and squinted inside. Stubbs put a quilted mitten in his hand. Bohannon peeled foil off a beef, green pepper, noodle casserole, set it on a counter, shoveled it onto a plate. "This will be fine." He threw the skeptical-looking Stubbs a smile and carried the plate with a fork to the table. He sat down, began to eat—he was hungry—and a sheet of paper lying just outside the circle of light from the lamp in the center of the table caught his eye. "What's this?"

"T. Hodges was here tonight." Stubbs brought a mug of coffee to the table, sat down with a suppressed groan. "She stayed almost an hour, hoping you'd show up." He pried a bent cigarette from a crumpled pack, lit it with a kitchen match. "Finally says she had to go, and wrote you that."

The handwriting was just what he'd have expected of the deputy—firm and without flourishes, straight up and down, easy to read. It said a woman's dog had been struck and its leg broken on Pleasant Trail this morning early. Pleasant Trail was where Alice Donovan's shop was. And the woman lived across and just down the road from there. She said the car that hit the dog was a new red Suzuki Samurai but she didn't get the license number. It came out of the driveway at Ye Olde Oak Tree hell-for-leather, and caromed down the dusty little road. The driver was a tall, young-looking man with a deep tan and a trim little beard. The woman, Gladys Tyndall, didn't know him, never saw him before. But she would like to get her hands on him. Her dog was going to be okay, but he could as easily be dead for all that driver cared.

Bohannon scraped the fork around on the plate for the last taste of his supper. "That was good," he said. "Hardly dried out at all. Thank you, George."

Stubbs grunted. "You want some coffee now?"

"Any of that blueberry cobbler of yours left?"

Stubbs brought the cold cobbler and a mug of hot coffee. Bohannon got up and trudged to the sideboard for a whiskey bottle, came back with it, added a jolt of whiskey to his coffee, and sat down. He picked up T. Hodges' note and rattled it at Stubbs. "You know any young man with a trimmed beard, a suntan, who drives one of those new little Japanese jeeps?"

"I thought you'd never ask," Stubbs said. He twisted out his smoked-down cigarette in the big glass ashtray on the table.

"Him and that red-haired tall girl been up here a couple times to ride the trails."

"Her name"—Bohannon had a mouthful of cobbler; he swallowed, gulped some coffee—"is Andrea Norse. What's his?"

"Beats me," Stubbs said. "It was her that signed in."

"So her address is in our records," Bohannon said.

"If it ain't," Stubbs said, "I'm slipping, and I better start thinking about the old folks' home."

Bohannon got to his feet and went into the shadows for the scuffed gray cardboard box of file cards.

The Samurai stood high on its wheels under drooping blue wisteria beside a rickety white frame cottage among a lot of others like it. This was one of the earliest spots built up in Settlers Cove. Bohannon got down from his truck, ducked under the wisteria, which showered him with dew. He pulled open an aluminum screen door and rapped at a brightly varnished wooden door. It was just past seven in the morning. So quiet he could hear the surf breaking, many streets away. Nobody stirred inside the house. He lit a cigarette and knuckled the door again, harder this time. After a ten-second pause, he heard the thump of footfalls, and the tall, redheaded girl opened the door, tugging down a big, loose sweater, shaking back her hair. She had on tight jeans and was barefoot. She winced in the morning light.

"What is it?"

"You know the owner of this vehicle?" Bohannon had his wallet out and open to show his license. He closed the wallet and pushed it away. "It struck a dog yesterday morning about this time, over on Pleasant Trail."

She looked wary. "Who are you, exactly?"

He told her. "Working for the public defender. On the Alice Donovan case? Did you know her, Miss Norse?"

She paled. "I—yes, I counseled her son, Howard." Her smile was thin and didn't last. "He had problems."

"You didn't counsel his mother?" Bohannon said. "Wasn't she behind those problems?"

Her tone hardened. "She didn't see it that way."

"That's how I see it." Bohannon gave her his best smile. "Don't you agree with me?"

"It's very early in the morning, Mr. Bohannon. I have to get ready for work. If you'll excuse me—"

"The Samurai is not your car, is it?" he said.

A bearded young man, naked to the waist, buttoning brown walking shorts, came to the door. His dark hair was tousled from sleep. He blinked and yawned. He was tall enough to reach over Andrea Norse's head and take hold of the door she was holding open. "What's this all about?" he said.

Bohannon told him about the dog. "What's your name?"

"Wolfe. I'm sorry about the dog. I didn't know I'd hit anything. I'll pay the woman."

"You didn't know you hit anything because you came tearing out of Alice Donovan's driveway in a sweat. Why? What were you doing there? Why did you kick in her back door? What was it you were after?"

Wolfe squinted. "Who's Alice Donovan?"

Looking mournful, Andrea Norse touched his chest. "It's no use, Zach. He knows we know her." She turned to face Bohannon. "We heard on the early-morning radio news that Alice had been murdered. I was over there the night before, to plead with her to change her tactics with Howard. I'd tried before. Howard used to come to me in tears."

"Drunken tears?" Bohannon said.

"Not always, but always heartbroken. That sunny little woman. She was a monster, you know. Sex-starved, smothering, seductive—as mixed up and dangerous as they come."

"Should I quote you on that?" Bohannon twitched her a half smile. "It doesn't sound exactly clinical."

"No." She looked ashamed of herself. "But I couldn't stand by and not try to change the situation. She was destroying her own son. He was very disturbed when he came to this door night before last."

"So disturbed he killed her," Wolfe said, and swung away. "I need coffee."

"I don't think so," Bohannon said. And to the Norse woman, "So you went over to try to talk to her? When?"

"Howard stayed here spilling out his woes to me for hours. When I'd got him calmed down and he left, I drove over to Madrone. What time? Ten? A little past."

"And she was all right?" Bohannon said.

"Self-righteous, smug, superior. Did I think you learned about human nature from books? What was I—thirty years old? Had I raised children of my own? She tried to keep him straight. But he wasn't bright, and boys like that awful Beau Larkin kept getting him into trouble."

"You knew Howard. Could he have killed her?"

"She was his god. We don't kill our gods."

"She wasn't your god. You didn't use that skillet?"

"No, of course not. I'd taken Howard's case folder with me—his history. I wanted to go through it point by point, episode by episode, to show her just how she—"

"And she wouldn't listen, and you walked out," Bohannon said, "and in your anger you left the file behind, and the next morning you remembered, and sent Zach to get it before the sheriff could connect you to the killing."

"He got it," she said wryly, "but it seems it didn't help. What am I now? Under arrest for murder?"

Bohannon shook his head. "I don't arrest people. I just ask questions. Can you prove you weren't there at midnight? What time did you get home? Was anyone here?"

"Zach and a friend, Sonny Snyder. When? Eleven? Zach put *Diva* on the VCR. He knows it always calms me down."

Bohannon turned away. "Tell him to stop in at the sheriff's about the dog before he goes to work." He ducked under the wisteria. In the road he dropped his cigarette and stepped on

it. And a bullet slammed into his shoulder. He heard the report
of the rifle as he fell. It echoed off the hills. A second shot
kicked grit into his face but that was all. Then Zach Wolfe was
kneeling beside him.

"It's all right," he said, "I'm a doctor."

Gerard said, "We'll handle it from now on. Okay?" He sat on
a chrome-and-wicker chair in a hospital room. Clear noon sunlight fell on him from a window. It gleamed off his scalp. Gerard
was developing a bald spot. Bohannon hadn't noticed that before. He sat up in the high bed, left arm in a sling, lunch on a
tray in front of him. He laid the fork down. The food was tepid
and tasteless.

"Did you let Howard go? Obviously, he didn't shoot me."

Gerard shrugged. "Alice was blackmailing people. You were
tracking those people down. It made somebody nervous. It
doesn't change Howard's status."

"More than nervous," Bohannon said. "Deadly."

"We found the shell casings up the hillside in a tangle of
brush and ferns and trees. They could have come from a thousand rifles around here. Thirty-thirty. No dwellings up there.
We can't find anybody who saw him."

Bohannon stuck with his thought. "If he was willing to kill
me, he was willing to kill Alice Donovan."

"It wasn't Dr. Worthy." Gerard pushed back the crisp cuff
of his tan uniform shirt to read his watch. "It wasn't Mrs.
Weems." He stood up. "That was sharp of you, having Andrea
Norse check on them right then by phone."

"Oh, I'm a hee-ro, I am. Lying there bleeding in the dust
and gasping out orders with my dying breath."

"Don't let it go to your head." Gerard opened the door.
From the hallway came the squeak of nurses' shoe soles, the
jingle of medication trays, the clash of lunch dishes being collected. "Fred May wants us to give you a medal."

"He was here earlier," Bohannon said. "He feels worse than
I do about it. He takes things hard."

"We'll find who did it," Gerard said.

"Unless I find him first," Bohannon said.

Gerard turned back. "You stay where you are, damn it. It's the only way we can protect you." He spoke to the young deputy posted on a chair outside Bohannon's door. "Don't let him trick you, Vern. He's sneaky."

Vern poked his fair-haired head around the door frame and grinned at Bohannon. "I'll watch him, sir," he said.

Looking half amused, half grim, Gerard went away.

The phone by the bed was almost as good as freedom. He rang T. Hodges to confirm a suspicion about the Kanter case. He rang Andrea Norse to bring the new truck down to the hospital. And Manuel Rivera, at the stables, to bring him clothes without bloodstains and a packet of little firecrackers that had lain in a drawer of the kitchen sideboard for years.

Rivera appeared in his soutane.

"Close the door," Bohannon told him. "Help me get dressed." It was tricky. There was the arm in the sling to work around and he was slow from the painkillers they'd given him. But they managed it. "Okay," he said. "Now, you open the door, say goodbye to me, go on down the hall and around the corner, then light the firecrackers, drop them, and walk out as if you had nothing to do with it."

Rivera regarded him with doubtful brown eyes.

"It will work," Bohannon said. "Who's going to suspect a priest?"

"No one will be harmed?" Rivera asked.

"It will just make a racket."

"I don't feel good about it," Rivera said.

"Do it anyway," Bohannon said. "A postulant should learn what it's like to sin. Manuel, go on. It's important."

The slim lad sighed, shook his head, but he went.

Bohannon's only worry was that the firecrackers were so old they wouldn't go off. But they did. A few of them, and made sufficient noise to send Vern racing down the hall and out of sight. Bohannon went in the other direction. He found the truck with the keys in it in the parking lot. By the time he was rolling down the street, his shoulder had begun to throb. But he was under way. He laughed to himself.

He could hear the music a block off when he halted the truck at a stop sign. The neighborhood was one of ranch-style houses on comfortable lots with well-grown trees. How were they taking that clamor—the thud of drums, the snarl of electric guitars? And the crowd noises that went with it, shouts, raucous laughter, four-letter words? The street was parked up, too. How did the neighbors like that? He turned a corner, found an alley, parked there, and entered the uproar through a back gate. The rock music hit him like an eighteen-wheeler.

The crowd he could see was all male, teenage, college-age, town boys, ranch boys, jeans, surfer trunks, work shoes, jogging shoes, baseball caps, straw hats, and crazily shaved heads with no hats at all. They stamped their feet to the roaring music, howled and whooped, pushed and tripped each other. At a brick outdoor barbecue a fat boy scorched hamburger patties. Beside the grill a plastic tub held beer cans on ice. Empty cans kicked around underfoot. Everybody had a can in his hand except three boys who lay passed out on the grass. The smell of mesquite smoke was strong in the windless air of the hot afternoon. But so was the smell of marijuana.

Nobody noticed Bohannon. He looked around for the kid hosting this shindig. He would stand out. He was almost as big as Howard Donovan. Then Bohannon saw him. He came out the back door of the house, surrounded by squealing girls, carrying hamburger buns, ketchup, mustard, barbecue sauce. Drunken cheers went up as they pushed through the crowd toward the red-faced fat boy in the smoke. Bohannon followed, and waited until the girls scattered. He poked the big boy's ribs. Beau Larkin swung around and stared at him. The color drained from his face. He licked his lips. He stammered.

"Hey, where did you come from?"

"Come on." Bohannon caught his arm and hauled him out the back gate into the alley.

"You can't touch me, my father's a police officer."

"And he was on the Kanter robbery case, that collection of Navajo Indian jewelry. And one piece disappeared from the collection. I know your father. He's an honest cop. He didn't take it. I think you took it. And tried to sell it to Alice Donovan, only she recognized it for what it was, and she's been blackmailing you with it ever since. Making you pay her not to tell your father."

Larkin reeked of beer. He peered glassily down at Bohannon. He swayed. His speech was slurred. "Howard said she'd buy it off me. I didn't know where else to go."

"Why did you kill her, Beau?"

"Because I was behind on my payments. My old man got sore and cut off my cash flow. I couldn't pay her. But she didn't care. She was going to tell him. I had to kill her. I thought I was out of trouble. But then you got the thing from where she had it hid. Cassie at the café told Tony about this stolen Indian buckle you had, and he told me. And I heard how smart you are, and I knew you'd be after me soon. So I had to kill you, too. And now I have to do it again." He lunged. His big hands grabbed Bohannon's throat.

Bohannon struggled. His shoulder screamed pain. He put an open hand against the boy's face and pushed. He kicked. He kneed. Nothing helped. The boy's thumbs were cutting off his air. The light was going out. His ears rang. Then a shout sliced through the backyard noise. A gun went off. Larkin let him go, and Bohannon staggered a few steps, gasping, choking, until his legs wouldn't hold him. He slumped against a fence, and blurrily saw Larkin lying face down in weeds and cinders, and Vern bending over, snapping handcuffs on the boy's thick wrists.

"Hack, were you crazy?" T. Hodges made the rocker in Bohannon's pine-plank bedroom creak angrily. "Going after a giant like that—with only one good arm, just out of surgery? How did you expect to even get there?"

He lay in his own bed. That was the good part. The bad part was how sore his throat was. He couldn't swallow food. It even hurt to talk. The sound that came out was hoarse, no more than a whisper. "It's over now. Calm down."

"You were lucky Vern got there when he did."

Vern gave his toothy kid grin. "Lieutenant Gerard warned me he was tricky." He stood gangly at the foot of the poster bed. "Soon as I saw those firecrackers, I knew it was Mr. Bohannon back of it. He didn't get much of a start on me. Broke a lot of speed laws, though. With that old patrol car I had, I almost lost him a couple of times."

"I was drugged," Bohannon whispered, "didn't know what I was doing." He heard voices in the hallway and looked at the door. Fred May came in, wearing a pup-tent-size pink sweatshirt that had once been red. He did his best to smile, but worry for how Bohannon felt spoiled the attempt. As if Bohannon were hovering near death, he looked for advice to the two young deputies.

"Is it okay?" he said. "I brought somebody."

"Fred, I'm all right." Bohannon hoped he was more successful with his try at smiling than May had been. "Who is it?"

Who it was filled the doorway. Howard Donovan. He held there, shy as a five-year-old, trying to find the words to thank Bohannon for getting him out of jail. "They all thought I killed my mother." Tears brimmed his eyes, and he used big fists to knuckle the tears away. "You knew I didn't do that. You knew I wouldn't."

"I was betting on it."

Howard grinned unexpectedly. "Even if I did pick you up that night and throw you in the water."

"It's not the same," Bohannon said.

"That was only funning, wasn't it?" Howard said. He looked grave again. "She made me very mad sometimes, but I wouldn't hurt her. I never did hurt her. Even when she hit me. Not once." He frowned to himself. "It wouldn't be right. She was too little." He paused, and abruptly the small boy that lived in his head changed the subject. Excited. Eyes shining. "There's a big old owl up in our tree. Did you know that? And the crows been pestering him."

"Yes," Bohannon said, "I knew that."

"Well, guess what? When I came home from jail, there's black feathers all over the yard. Crow feathers. Guess that old owl showed them who's boss, didn't he?"

"It's his tree," Bohannon said. "We both knew that."

"And it's my house," Howard said. "Isn't it?"

Molly's Aim

The town of Poinsettia waits among brown rolling hills under a high, wide, blue California sky for something to happen. And it never will. That's how Molly feels. It never will. Time stands still here. Poised on a corner now, waiting for one of the little town's two stoplights to change—Main Street is a state highway, and strangers can come speeding out of the hills and around the curve and be surprised by the town—she looks up and down the street and sees the same dowdy one- and two-story brick store buildings she's seen her whole life long here, all thirty years of it.

Two cars streak past, filled with kids bound for the Consolidated High School. They shriek and laugh. Arms wave out of windows. A soda-pop can goes flying. Molly aches for a moment at the sight, the sounds. She wishes she were back in high school. Those were the good times. The light changes, and she crosses the street.

The Sleep EZ motel is tucked back among old eucalypts with thick, twisted trunks at the south end of town. She has worked here ten years already. And she can't see how she'll ever leave. The door to the office is plate glass. She pushes inside. A bald head is visible behind the wood-grain plastic counter. Molly says cheerily, "Good morning, Mr. Gobineau."

He wakes with a snort, blinks at her, pushes to his feet. It must take effort. He is a big-bellied man. "Ten o'clock already?" He winces at the daylight pouring in through the glass door. "Another fine day, I see."

"The ranchers want rain." Molly studies the registration cards in a loose-leaf contraption on the counter to learn the numbers of the occupied units. From the automobiles on the weedy tarmac of the parking area, she knows how many. Five. It's been a quiet night.

She glances at the vinyl-tile floor of the office. A quick damp mopping will do for it. Checking for dust and disorder, she eyes the fake-leather chairs, the wood-grain plastic coffee table with its vase of plastic flowers, ragged travel magazines, ashtray. Some dog has streaked the glass door with its nose. After she changes from her jeans and sweater into white smock and trousers, she will take spray cleaner and paper towels to the door. She wants to keep busy until checkout time at eleven, when she can get into the units, clean up after the guests, change the bedding and towels.

But now she frowns. Has she really seen that name? She turns back to the registration cards. Her small hands flip them over swiftly. There. Is she right about that name? She traces the letters with a finger. She never really got the hang of reading. She must be wrong. *Hugh Henderson?* She makes a little sound. She's dizzy. Her knees feel weak. She catches the edge of the counter to steady herself.

Mr. Gobineau's brows rise. "What's the matter? You're pale. Are you sick?"

She gives him what she knows must be a wan little smile. "I'm just a little dizzy."

What shall she do? She isn't ready. For twelve years she's wished for this to happen, wished so fiercely she sometimes thought she'd die from wanting it—that Hugh Henderson would return to Poinsettia. Now it's happened, and she has no plans.

"Sit down," Mr. Gobineau says. "I'll call Mrs. Gobineau. Here"—the big green Arrowhead bottle back of the counter gurgles and he passes her a paper cup of water—"drink this." He lumbers away, panicked, calling, "Marie, come quickly— Molly's sick!"

Molly doesn't drink the water, doesn't sit down. She stands at the counter, her heart beating heavily, thickly. Her voice sounds strange and high to her as she asks Mr. Gobineau's worried old face, "Hugh Henderson—why did he stop here? Why not at his mother's house? His house. Where he grew up?"

"Henderson?" Gobineau squints at the registry card. "Ah, that young man. Well, it was late when he arrived. Perhaps he didn't want to awaken his mother."

"She died," Molly says. "Day before yesterday."

"Ah, then he's here for the funeral," Mr. Gobineau says. He peers at her. "You know him?"

Molly must be careful. She's already said too much. She stammers quickly, "No, not really. We—we went to high school together is all."

Mr. Gobineau cocks a sly eyebrow. "You're blushing. He was your childhood sweetheart, no?"

She laughs. She can't help it. Little scrawny Hugh, with his big brown eyes in a face that even when he was a high school senior looked like a ten-year-old girl's? What a silly idea. It was tall, strapping, fair-haired Carl Wynant who was Molly's sweetheart. For a dreamy moment now, she glows with re-membered pride in that. Then the old black rage rises in her, so strongly that she feels dizzy again.

Motherly little Mrs. Gobineau hurries in and Molly gives her a wan smile. "I—I'm sorry. I didn't have such a good night. The pizza I ate or something." She turns for the door, acting weaker than she really feels. "I'd better—better go home and rest today." Hand on the door, she turns back. "Can you man-age without me?"

Mrs. Gobineau waddles to her, gives her a hug with her soft fat arm, her pillowy old face wrinkled with concern. "Yes, yes, I'll manage, *ma petite*. You stop at the doctor. Telephone us. Tell us how you are."

"Thank you," Molly says, and pushes out into the warm sunshine.

She's frightened at having left work. She never did this to the Gobineaus before. She mustn't lose her job. Who else would hire her? Not Snyder's Luncheonette. Mrs. Snyder died and the café's been sold. The Snyders and the Gobineaus didn't care that Molly can't read or write or figure and has to have things explained to her so often. When the Gobineaus are gone, who else will be so patient and kind? What will become of Molly if she loses the friendship of the Gobineaus?

She stops at her corner and stands breathing quickly, excited, frightened, watching for speeding cars. It can't be helped. She needs time to think and plan. Anyway, at the motel, Hugh might see her and that could ruin everything. She crosses the street and, padding along quickly in her soft-soled shoes, makes for the haven of her rooms, where she can be alone and decide what to do.

Her mind has never been quick. As a girl, it had hurt her when other girls said so, made fun of her, called her Molly the Moron. Time has taught her that, though cruel, they were right. She is not clever. If she'd been clever, Carl would never have been able to trick her as he did. But—she sets her jaw and works the latch of the wire-mesh gate to the yard of old grapefruit trees—she can get even with him now.

She closes the gate and walks up the cement strip beside an old white-frame house to a side door at the rear and her little apartment. Inside, in her tiny kitchen, she takes a Coke from the shivery old fridge, sits down at the paint-faded table, and lights a cigarette. She pops the top of the dewy can and swallows some of the cold, sweet, tingly drink. If she takes her time now, she can make a plan. She has no choice. Her chance has come at last, and it may be the only one she ever gets. She frowns, trying to concentrate.

But her thinking is all a jumble. She jumps up impatiently, goes to the window over the chipped sink, stares out at the only view, the side of the neighbor's paint-scaly garage. If she can't think, she can remember. Sometimes she wishes she couldn't. But remember she can and does.

If she's lucky, her memories are of the happy high school times. There had been boys. They never mocked her as the girls did. They bought her beers and fried chicken, and took her to drive-in movies in their cars, and out into the hills—or sometimes even to the far-off beach—to make love afterward. And if this one didn't ask her a second time, there'd soon be another, and another. She loved high school.

Her childhood had been a nightmare. After her mother died, her father snarled at her sober and hit her when he was drunk. She didn't want to anger him, but she couldn't understand what he wanted. His temper made her jumpy, and she kept breaking things and breaking rules and not living up to her mother. Not in looks, not in brains, not in anything. Except her aim with a gun. He was proud of that—when he remembered it, which was less and less often as time went by.

Molly was worst of all at cooking. The meals she fixed on her own her father pushed away. Sometimes he threw the plate at her. She took to heating TV dinners. And grew grateful for the times, more and more common as the years passed, when he snored unshaven, mouth hanging open, unconscious from whiskey in his chair facing the television set, or felt too awful even to get out of his bed, sometimes for days at a time.

But this meant he couldn't get work. He was good and quick and sure at fixing up whatever needed mending—plumbing, wiring, roofing—on ranches and in town. But he got so unreliable, promising to show up and not showing up until days later, that finally the phone stopped ringing.

A trickle of money came every month from a tiny trust fund of her mother's, but it wasn't enough, so Molly had to take work to bring in extra. A half-crippled old widower, Morgan Dowd, had her in for a couple of hours after school every other day to dust and vacuum his big empty old house, do the laundry, wash up the dishes, scrub the bathrooms, shop for groceries, pick up his prescriptions from the drugstore.

She had one dream in those grim years. To escape.

First she'd escaped into heavy makeup and flashy costume jewelry from Woolworth's, into dresses too old for her, into smoking, flirting, drinking beer and wine, talking sexy with the boys. Into having sex with the boys, when she learned that was what drew them. Other girls were prettier, other girls had better families, nicer houses, more money, even cars of their own, other girls got better grades. But the boys liked Molly and she liked the boys.

Still, she hadn't been prepared for Carl Wynant. Carl was the star of the football team, captain of the basketball team, a four-hundred hitter in baseball. On the big campus of the Consolidated High School, among a thousand kids from all over this side of the county, he was the best known. He could have had the company of pretty girls, rich girls, girls who got all A's. But it was Molly Byrne he picked.

In the cafeteria at lunch one day when it was raining so hard no one had gone off campus to get decent food—pizza or burritos or Big Macs—she asked him why. She knew it was dumb of her even as the question came out of her mouth between bites of meatloaf and mashed potatoes. A girl should be grateful for a miracle like Carl and not mess with his head. But not knowing was driving her wild. She had to ask him. He stared at her for a minute, surprised, and then he laughed. She felt cold. Was he laughing at her?

He swallowed the food in his mouth, gulped milk, and grinned at her. "They don't really want me, Molly. They just want to show the other girls they can corner the big man on campus. I'm a trophy. They're hunters."

"I think you're great," Molly said.

"I'm not. I'm good at sports, that's all. And what is this?" He gestured to take in not just the wide, chattery, clattery cafeteria, but the campus and all its buildings. "High school in the boonies. I'm a star here, but I wouldn't be nothing at a school with real competition."

"You could be anything you want, Carl," she said.

He wiped his mouth with a paper napkin and crumpled it into a ball, tossing it at the head of a boy seated across the room. It hit its mark, and the boy looked around to see where it came from, but couldn't see. Carl snorted laughter and turned to Molly, sober again. "None of those girls would dream of marrying me, Molly."

"Why not? Of course they would."

He counted on his strong fingers. "I'm poor, I got no background, I got no future—"

Molly took his hand, squeezed it, looked into his blue, blue eyes. "I don't think that's true. But even if it is, I still love you."

He nodded and stood. "We're two of a kind." He picked up his dishes, piled them on her tray, and picked up her tray. "Come on," he said. "I need you, Molly. Right now."

She scurried after him. "But the rain, Carl."

"I've got the truck today," he said.

It was a ratty old truck with fading red paint and a scaling sign on its doors: WYNANT'S EGGS. It smelled of chickens. She knew where he was taking her. Copenhagen—the hulking barn of a deserted ranch where the house had long ago burned down. The barn bore on one side a weather-bleached advertisement for Copenhagen snuff. She didn't know what snuff was, or Copenhagen, either, but Copenhagen was what they called the place. Carl wasn't the only one who knew about it—it was whispered about among the older students, giggled about, but she knew of no one else who ever actually used it. Carl called it his place, and she went along with his make-believe. It made her feel warm inside.

It wasn't warm inside the barn. It was cold and damp. They climbed to the haymow up a splintery ladder. The rain pattered softly on the shingles. Carl crossed deep straw and dug the rolled-up sleeping bag from a corner. It was the kind with zippers all around so it could be spread out. Its black satiny lining always felt luscious on her skin.

They undressed each other, stopping for long kisses, long fondlings, shivering in the weather but not noticing that they were shivering, warmed from within themselves by the heat of their blood. They dropped, already joined where they both craved wildly to be joined, onto the padded, satiny bed on the deep, springy straw.

Afterward, Carl turned away for an instant and stretched an arm to get cigarettes from his cast-off jacket, lit one for himself, one for her, and lay naked, blond, shining, hair in his eyes, leaning up on an elbow, looking down at her thoughtfully. "You really like it," he said. "You like doing all the different things, don't you?"

"All of them." She pushed up to kiss his smoky mouth. "Don't you?"

"Hell, yes, but that's different—boys are horny. Girls aren't supposed to be horny, you know."

"Who says?" she scoffed. Then she was grave again. "I love you, Carl."

"Same here." He got up off the sleeping bag and stood looking down at her. "I love you, too, Molly."

She knelt up and rubbed her face against his flat, hard belly. "You're wonderful."

He laughed softly, stroked her hair, and turned away to balance first on one leg, then the other, and pull on Jockey shorts. "What do you think?" he said, and drew a T-shirt on over his head. "Do you want us to be together forever?" He smoothed the shirt down.

"Can we?" She could hardly believe what he was asking. Her heart thudded. "Do you mean it?"

"Hell, yes." He kicked into his jeans. "Only not like this. Not here, Molly, not in Poinsettia. Not with your drunk father. Not with my mother and her damn ten thousand chickens and nothing ahead but eggs and more eggs forever." He zipped up the jeans. "With maybe ten dollars between us for a Friday-night Chinese supper in Atascadero and a movie afterward."

He flapped into his checkered flannel shirt and poked the tails down into his pants. "I'm sick of being poor. I'm sick of working my ass off for nothing." He sat down to pull on thick white gym socks and then the short strapped motorcycle boots he always wore. "Aren't you sick of being poor?"

"Yes." She nodded. "Only, what can we do about it? I can't get a good job. I don't know anything. There's no money to send me to college. And if there was, I couldn't go. I'm a very poor student."

He laughed that grim laugh of his again. "Yeah, that's another way we're alike." He gathered up his jacket and walked to the ladder, the planks of the loft creaking under his weight. "Come on"—he looked at the watch they gave him after last year's football season—"it's after three. My mom will chew me out. And you'll be late to old man Dowd's." He started down the ladder. "You know what they say? He's got money hidden all over that house." He made a heavy thump as he landed on the barn floor below. "Is it true, Molly?"

"People make up stories," she said.

"Maybe not," he called up to her. "Why don't you nose around and find out?"

Molly now almost believes she did eat tainted pizza last night. She feels a little nauseated and goes to lie on her bed. It makes up into a sofa if she wants, but ordinarily she doesn't do the stowing of pillows and heavy lifting needed to make the bed part disappear. She gets enough of that kind of work at the Sleep EZ, and she's usually tired when she comes home.

At the motel, when she's cleaning the rooms, she almost always switches on the television sets. She could switch her own set on now. But she doesn't. She just pries off her shoes, lies down in her jeans and sweater, puts two pillows under her head, and gazes at the leaf-shadowed open window, where a hot breeze moves the half-drawn roller shade so it ticks against the frame.

And she thinks of Hugh Henderson, who has come home to

bury his mother. It never came to Molly that Mrs. Henderson would die. Why not? Everybody dies at last. And mostly when they do, their relations—certainly their sons and daughters—come home. But maybe because nothing good ever happens to her she'd settled in her mind that Hugh Henderson wouldn't. True, what happened was a long time ago—but because so little ever does happen in Poinsettia, when there's a scandal people remember, and Hugh would know that. Yet come home he has. She can't believe her luck.

But how is she going to take advantage of it? She scowls. It's back to planning again, isn't it? And her mind shies from the assignment. The thought of it wears her out before she can begin. Instead, she slides once more into remembering—this time how it came about that little Hugh Henderson, who had adored big Carl Wynant, came to hate him. . . .

For a long while, that spring term of 1977, he tagged Carl around—in the school hallways, across the campus under the oaks and pepper trees. He was always there, sitting alone, a frail figure on the forsaken bleachers snapping picture after picture of Carl at afternoon batting practice, footracing, jumping hurdles on the gravel track—even, Molly was told, in the locker room, hanging around among the big, shower-sleek bodies of the athletes. That camera around his neck seemed part of Hugh. He wore it everywhere, every day, all day.

Toward the end, he and Carl began to eat lunch together, to drive together in Carl's truck to movies in Paso Robles or Santa Maria on Friday and Saturday nights. At least once, they traveled to the coast on a Sunday—they were seen sailing at Morro Bay. Then somebody started the rumor that they were gay. Flowers appeared in Carl's locker with a card signed *To Carl with all my love—Hugh*. The girls all chattered and giggled about it.

Then someone stole the white stuff they used to draw lines on the football field and printed out there in letters four feet high CARL WYNANT LOVES HUGH HENDERSON with a heart with an arrow through it. The coaches pretended to make a big fuss about this, but they never caught who did it. They tried to rub out the words, wash them out with hoses, but the words stayed till next fall's football games scuffed them away. And the coaches grinned. They thought it was funny, too. Anyone could see that.

Carl didn't grin. He hated being laughed at. He hated being called queer. The next Saturday night, he filled the truck with his best jock friends and picked up Hugh. They took him out in the hills and stripped him and made him do things to them, and did things to him, and then brought him back and dumped him, kicked, beaten, bleeding, and stark naked, in the center of town, in front of the post office and the lighted stores, and drove off. A lot of people were still awake and saw Hugh stumbling miserably home through the streets. They weren't scandalized at what had happened to him. They were scandalized because he didn't have any clothes on.

The sheriff questioned Carl and the other boys, but they wouldn't tell on each other and no one was arrested. But at Snyder's Luncheonette—where Molly, even though she couldn't write down the orders or add up the checks, sometimes helped out if Wilma Snyder was sick—the breakfasters agreed it was Carl and his friends who'd done it. And Carl himself told Molly about it the next year, one of those good times when they lay naked in the dark. At first it frightened her to know Carl could do such a thing, but she soon forgot about it. He wasn't cruel, he was only protecting his reputation. He wasn't gay. Those other boys forced him to prove it.

And Hugh wasn't killed, after all, only bruised and shamed. He left town, not waiting for the semester to end. His mother claimed not to know where he had gone. So no one could ask him how he felt. But Molly knew. He hated Carl, with the same betrayed fury Molly later came to feel, and still feels. She's had to keep her hatred secret, but everyone, including the sheriff, knows Hugh has to be Carl's enemy.

And now Hugh is back, and Molly can have her revenge on

Carl at last—if only she can figure out how to make the sheriff pin the blame on Hugh.

An hour later she's back in the kitchen, seated at the table, drinking another Coke and struggling to put a plan onto paper. It's old, unused notebook paper from her high school days. She rarely put anything on paper then, and it's hard for her to form words now. She does it like a kindergartner, one crooked letter at a time. She thought it would help keep her mind from wandering. And maybe it has a little. It's also given her a headache.

CARL, she has printed, HUGH, MOLLY, and CARL'S COME-ON-INN. She has drawn lines radiating out from these last words so it will look as if they're shining like the sign on top of Carl's roadhouse on the highway outside town. She has rung Information and written down the telephone numbers of the nightclub and the Henderson house. But none of it gets her anyplace.

The one thing that makes her feel that somehow what she must do she is going to do is the 30-30 rifle she's pulled out of the back of a closet, dusted off, cleaned, oiled, and loaded. It now stands leaning against the side of the stove, the rifle she bought quietly in San Luis Obispo to replace her father's, which she lost on that most terrible night of all her life, twelve years ago. The new rifle cost her all her pitiful savings, and she was scared to death her father would discover it wasn't his gun, but he was so drunk most of the time she could only hope he wouldn't notice—and he didn't. Or if he did, he never said so.

When she and Carl lay on the sleeping bag again in the loft at Copenhagen, she told him how, the day before, when it turned cold in the late afternoon, she'd gone back to Mr. Dowd's house to fetch the coat she'd forgotten and there in the dining room was the old man, down on his bony knees, a corner of the carpet folded back, prying up a square of the parquet floor. He took out a fishing-tackle box, opened it, and pushed paper money into it, quite a thick stack, to lie on top of stacks already in the box. Not then—they had other things to occupy them then—but when they were driving back to town in the egg truck, they planned what they would do. As she climbed down out of the truck at her front gate, Carl leaned across the seat and told her in a loud whisper, "Bring your father's gun."

She slid it from under her father's bed, where he'd sprawled in his filthy clothes, whiskery, reeking of drink, snoring like a pig. It never occurred to her to ask what they would need with a gun. She took it because that was what Carl said to do. She had a key, of course, and when she softly unlocked the back door of Mr. Dowd's tall house on its ten-acre lot that cold night and they tiptoed into the dark kitchen, Carl was carrying the gun in one gloved hand.

Molly's heart pounded with fright. It made a roaring in her ears so she could hardly hear. Not that there was much to hear—crickets out in the darkness, now and then a car droning along the distant highway. The neighborhood was asleep, the town was asleep. Carl groped for her hand and she guided him into the dining room, where the long, polished table, its erect and empty chairs, and the big mirrored sideboard were no more than darker chunks of the darkness.

"Where?" Carl whispered.

Mutely, on trembling legs, Molly led him to the corner where a little side table held a clutch of silver vessels—coffeepot, sugar bowl, and cream pitcher—on a silver tray. They glinted in the starlight through the windows. One of Molly's duties was to polish them once a month, though they were never used. No one came to dinner at the Dowd house, not after Mrs. Dowd died.

"Show me," Carl whispered.

Molly knelt, and pushed his legs so he stepped aside. She folded back the corner of the carpet. "There," she whispered back and jumped up as quickly as if she'd uncovered a snake. She didn't want to touch the square of flooring.

Carl did. He handed her the rifle. She cradled it in her arm, as her father had taught her, and Carl knelt and felt around with his hands.

The next minute she heard a little squeak and saw a square hole open at his knees. He laid the patch of flooring aside, reached down, and lifted out the fishing-tackle box. It wasn't locked. He opened it, pawed inside, laughed a soft laugh, straightened up. And his head struck the table. The silver pieces rattled. The coffeepot teetered and gonged on the bare floor.

"Who's there?"

It was Mr. Dowd's voice. He wasn't upstairs. He was very near. Molly heard his slippers scuffing across the hallway into the living room, only a few paces away. He walked with a cane and couldn't get downstairs fast, so he must have been lying awake and heard the truck arrive, heard them enter the kitchen.

In his bathrobe and slippers, his thin gray hair mussed from sleep, he was pointing the beam of a flashlight around. "Who's there?" he said again in his high, trembly voice. Then the flashlight beam caught her full in the face and held her. "Molly? Is that you?"

Carl clapped a hand over her mouth, and somehow the gun went off. It made a terrible noise and gave a terrible kick that bruised her arm. She dropped it, but the harm was done—Mr. Dowd lay on his back in the gaping black opening to the living room. His dropped flashlight showed a dark stain spreading on his chest. He didn't make a sound.

Carl pushed her out of his way, ran to the old man, and knelt beside him. He picked up the flashlight and shone it on his face, touched the scrawny neck, grabbed a limp wrist, held it for a minute, and dropped it. He turned and looked at Molly. "You've killed him." He stuffed the flashlight in a pocket of his jacket and came striding back to her. He grabbed her and shook her so hard it seemed her head would snap off. "You've killed him! What the hell did you do that for?"

"I—I didn't mean to," Molly gabbled. "The gun just went off! The light was in my eyes and the gun just went off!"

"Yeah, wonderful." Carl flung her backward. She struck the little table, and the other silver pieces clattered to the floor. She stood huddled against the wall, looking at him wide-eyed.

He crouched, grabbing up the metal box and the rifle. "You stupid cow. I should have known you were too dumb for this."

"Carl, don't," she begged. "It was an accident."

He went to her, pushed his face close to hers, furious. "It was murder in the course of a robbery. You get the death penalty for that, Molly—they put you in the gas chamber."

Molly reached out to him. "No, Carl. I didn't mean it."

He slapped her hands away. "Don't touch me." He held up the box. "We were going to have a great life. I'll bet there are thousands in here, Molly. We could have gone anywhere, done anything."

"We still can." She turned toward the kitchen swing door. "Let's go, Carl. Like we planned."

"Oh, no"—he caught her arm—"I don't want any part of you. I'm going alone. You worked for Dowd. You'll be the first one they suspect. You don't dare leave town."

Molly could only stare.

"They'd come straight after you, Molly. Anyway, you think I'm teaming up with a killer? You think I'd put my life in your hands?" He gestured with the gun barrel at the body on the floor. "After what you did? Think again. I'd have to sleep sometimes, Molly. Who says when I'm asleep, you wouldn't murder me and take it all for yourself? Oh, no. I'm going alone."

She shook her head in horrified protest. How could he be saying what he was saying? He yanked her against him—not lovingly, threateningly. "And if you got some idea of telling the sheriff about me, just remember I saw you kill the old man. And I've got the gun you did it with—your father's gun. They can match up the bullets. All I did was take the money. It was you that did the killing. You think you can remember that?"

He slammed open the swing door with a fist, dragged her with him through the kitchen, down the back steps and the long clod-stumbly orchard to the truck. "Come on, I'll drop you home." He yanked open the door, pushed her roughly up into the cab, and slammed the door. He walked around the truck, set the box on the gritty floor, dropped the gun in back of the seats, got in, and started the noisy engine.

"Take me with you, Carl," she begged. "You promised."

"That was before I knew you were a killer," he said.

She hiked back to Mr. Dowd's house after school the next day. It was one of her days to go there and clean for him and she had to act as if everything was the same as ever. Her legs felt weak when she climbed the back steps. She trembled all over when she stepped into the daylit kitchen and heard the silence of the house, and knew the reason for the silence.

She pulled out a chair at the kitchen table and sat down. She didn't want to go any farther. But she made herself. She pushed the swing door and entered the dining room. She looked at the fallen silver pieces, the folded-back corner of the rug, the square of flooring, the hole it had concealed. But she couldn't look at Mr. Dowd.

There was no way to get to the telephone but to pass him, though. She went to the opening, looking at the table and chairs, the sideboard, the windows, the ceiling, anything but the dead body in the opening. Feeling as if she might faint, she slipped past it, edging around the door frame, then ran through the living room, and in the hallway snatched up the receiver of the telephone on the table there and dialed zero.

"What was in there, Molly?" The bony sheriff tapped the edge of the hole in the floor with his boot. "Do you know?"

Molly shook her head.

"Hid money in there, did he?" The sheriff smiled—he had horsy teeth. His thick glasses glinted. "Old people get funny ideas sometimes. Don't trust banks. Stuff money all sorts of crazy places, you'd be surprised."

He turned to watch the young men who had come in a county ambulance load the stiff body of Mr. Dowd onto a stretcher and carry him down the living room and out of sight into the hallway. The front door opened and closed. The shoes of the men thumped across the hollow front porch and down the steps. The doors of the ambulance slammed.

"I don't know anything about it," Molly said.

"It looks as if Mr. Dowd caught the robber in the act and the robber shot him."

"I suppose so," Molly said.

"Mr. Dowd keep a gun, did he? Hunting rifle?"

"He did say sometimes he'd like to shoot the deer eating the bark off his fruit trees. Maybe he had a gun in a closet someplace, but he was old and sick. I guess he wouldn't be using it, would he?"

"Maybe when he heard the robber," the sheriff said, "he got it out of that closet, came downstairs with it, and the robber just took it away from him and shot him with it."

She looked at the floor. "That's terrible," she said.

"He should have phoned us, not tried to take care of it himself. I don't know when people will get that idea through their heads." The sheriff pushed back his flat-brimmed hat with one finger and studied her. "Old people that hide money in the house usually lock up tight at night. But we can't find any sign of a break-in. Robber just walked in. The front door was locked—downstairs windows, too. What about that, Molly? Did he usually leave the back door open?"

"It was always locked when I got here to work," she said. "He gave me a key to let myself in."

The sheriff's eyebrows went up. "Did he, now?" He tilted his head, blinking. "Have you got that key now?"

She showed it to him. He took it and turned it over in his fingers. "Lend this to anybody last night?"

She shook her head. "Can I go now?"

"In a minute." The sheriff pocketed the key. "Did he have any visitors lately? Strangers?"

"Nobody came but Dr. Keinplatz," she said.

"No delivery men, anybody like that?"

"I used his car and did his shopping for him," she said. "Groceries, drugstore. I did the laundry. I drove him to the bank. Nobody delivered anything, except the mailman."

"No repairman, gas, electricity, plumber?"

"Not that I ever saw."

"And you never told anyone he had money hidden here?"

"I didn't know," she said again. "Can I go now?"

"You got a boyfriend?" He showed his horsy teeth again. "Pretty girl like you must have a boyfriend."

She felt herself blush hotly and her heart began to pound. "I don't have time. I go to school, and keep house here, and wait tables at the café, and look after my father. I don't have time for boyfriends."

Into his pale, vague eyes behind the thick lenses came a pitying look. He patted her shoulder kindly. "Well, don't fret. You will have. Some rich young fella will see you one day at the café, decide he can't live without you, and take you off to the bright lights and the big city."

"I guess not," she said.

Mr. Dowd was buried—a very old sister-in-law from the Midwest came to see to all of it, a creaky little woman who left straight after the funeral. She and Molly were the only ones in the pews of the big, high-raftered Presbyterian church, and the only ones at the graveside.

Molly kept fearing that the sheriff would question her again. At home, she nervously peered out the front windows, expecting to see him coming up the walk, bony in his carefully pressed tan uniform. Or maybe he'd come banging in at the screen door of the café one morning and put handcuffs on her and drag her away to jail. She imagined him asking around the high school and finding some girl who'd tell him Molly had lied to him—she did have a boyfriend, and it was Carl Wynant. And then the sheriff would go to Carl's mother's chicken ranch and find out he had left town the very night Mr. Dowd was killed.

She would see the sheriff in his patrol car sometimes when she was out on the streets. He seemed to gaze at her long and thoughtfully. But he never said a word. If he noticed her noticing him, he'd nod and touch the brim of his hat. But every time she saw him, it made her jumpy. She lay awake worrying about the sheriff.

"What's the matter with you?" her father growled at her over the breakfast table. "You look half dead. If you don't stop running around all night with the boys, you'll end up pregnant. Well, when you do, don't expect any help from me."

That was a laugh. When had he ever helped her? Not since before her mother died and he started drinking. After that, she was the one who did all the helping. "I don't run around with any boys," she said. "That's over with."

"Glad to hear it," he sneered. "When you going to get another job? Only one creature I know can live on air, and that's an orchid—and we ain't neither one of us orchids."

Dully, she picked up his empty plate and carried it with hers to the sink. "I talked to the people at the EZ motel. It's hard for them to keep maids. They're always leaving to go home to Mexico. Maybe they'll take me on. They said they'd phone."

"Don't leave it up to them." Her father pushed up from his chair. "Keep going down there and reminding them."

"I will, Daddy," she said, and ran water into the sink.

She wondered what had become of Carl. Days slid into weeks, and weeks into months, but she couldn't get him out of her mind. Was it love or hate? It made her angry to admit it, after what he did to her, but she wanted to be with him again at Copenhagen. She couldn't forget him. Was he in Las Vegas, like he'd sometimes said? Wherever he was, she dreamed of getting on the Greyhound bus and going to look for him.

One Sunday, when she had time on her hands, she walked out to the chicken ranch and stood looking down the long, two-rut road at the small white house among walnut trees and the long, whitewashed chicken sheds behind it. In vast pens, hundreds of white chickens pecked the dust. She touched the crusty steel latch of the gate, urging herself to push it up, swing the gate open, walk down the road, knock at the door, and, when Mrs. Wynant appeared, ask if she'd heard from Carl.

But of course she couldn't do that, could she? Mrs. Wynant would wonder what business Carl was of dumb little Molly Byrne's, anyway. She might get suspicious and demand to know what Molly knew about Carl and why he'd run off with the truck that night. Women weren't easy, like men, like the sheriff. Women weren't soft in the head when it came to dealing with a young girl if she'd interfered with one of their menfolk. Molly was afraid of Mrs. Wynant, and after that long, hot walk out to the chicken ranch she dropped her hand from the gate, turned, and trudged emptily back home.

At last a thing happened she would never have believed. Carl came back to Poinsettia. She smiles wryly to herself now. It seemed as if she, the one who cared the most, was about the last person to hear of it. And no one told her—she overheard it. No one would think to tell her, she guessed. By now most of her high school class had left town. Those able to go to college were over to Cal Poly in San Luis, or at UC Santa Barbara, or at the agricultural college in Davis. The others had to leave, too—there were no jobs in Poinsettia, not for bright people. They scattered to Los Angeles or San Francisco. Molly was about the only one who stayed.

She was working at the Sleep EZ by now, but they wanted her more and more at Snyder's Luncheonette, because Wilma was sick more and more of the time, so Molly worked twelve to fourteen hours a day sometimes and got home only to fall exhausted into bed. No time to watch TV or even listen to the radio. And she never read the papers—they were too hard.

So she heard it from a table of women from the bank and the Highway Patrol office eating early breakfast and gossiping about how the deserted roadhouse outside town had been sold to Carl Wynant.

"Wynant's Eggs?" one of the women said.

The other nodded. "That's the one."

"I remember him," a hatchet-faced woman said. "Big blond boy. Football player at the high school. Got into some kind of trouble with the sheriff once."

"I never thought he'd amount to anything."

"Well," the first woman said, picking at her omelette, looking for more pieces of mushroom than there were, "you never can tell about youngsters. They grow up and surprise you."

"Where did he get the money? Could his mother afford to buy him a nightclub?"

One of the bank women laughed. "I handle her account. She can't save a dime. Just barely makes ends meet, poor woman, once she's paid the help. When she had a husband and son, it was different."

"Ranch hands won't work for their meals and a place to sleep anymore," the woman with the omelette said. "Those days are gone forever."

"Why should trash like that work," the hatchet-faced woman said, "when they can live on welfare?"

"Isn't that the truth," the others said.

Mr. Snyder, red-faced in his chef's hat and apron, behind a service window filled with steaming plates, called impatiently for Molly and she wasn't able to stay and listen anymore.

She waited in a latticework patio beside the newly painted road-house. Ferns were hung up in pots, and new banana trees and flowering shrubs were stuck into corners. New redwood planks were underfoot. A jacaranda tree spread feathery shadows on the deck. Lacy white-metal chairs with designs pierced in the seats surrounded round white-metal tables. She sat at one of the tables. She was the only one here. It was early afternoon.

But the grand opening of Carl's Come-On-Inn happened last Saturday night. She'd walked out, footsore, after Snyder's closed and seen the gravel parking area beside the highway filled with cars, dressed-up people going in and out, laughing and chattering in the glow of the big new sign on the roof. So she figured Carl would be along today. Now a rattling at the side door got her attention, and in a minute the door opened and a thin young Asian man in kitchen whites stood there, blinking in the sunlight. He seemed surprised to see her.

She got off the chair and hurried to him. "Please tell Mr. Wynant Molly Byrne wants to see him."

The man jerked his head. "He inside. You come in?"

"No. You tell him. I'll wait out here."

The man blinked at her, shrugged, turned, and was gone.

She went back to sit at the table again. Then Carl came out. He'd changed. His hair had been shoulder-length at school. Now it was cut short as a banker's. He wore a gold-embroidered red cowboy shirt, narrow-legged beige whipcords, tooled cowboy boots dyed maroon and purple. All this seemed cheerful, but he didn't look cheerful. He looked angry. He closed the door behind him and came to her, scowling. "What the hell are you doing here?"

"Why did you come back? You hated Poinsettia."

"Until I saw other places. Molly, what do you want?"

"To remind you that half of this should be mine." She had rehearsed just what she was going to say. It surprised her that she got it out. She was terribly frightened. "You said that money from Mr. Dowd would be ours together, Carl. That's what you said."

"I don't go partners with murderers," he said.

"I can tell the sheriff 'where your money came from," she said. "He's always watching me. He thinks I know who robbed Mr. Dowd."

Carl straightened sharply. He stepped to the latticework and peered toward the highway. In a minute, he turned back. "You're crazy, Molly. It's been years."

"He's still waiting for me to tell him," she said. "And I can, can't I? He asked if I had a boyfriend. I said no, but I can still tell him the truth. And he can check it out, too, with who was in school with us then. It wasn't the big secret you thought it was. They knew we went to Copenhagen. The sheriff will believe me when I say you were with me at Mr. Dowd's. And if it was you that ran off with the money, why wasn't it you that did the shooting?"

"It wasn't my gun. It was your old man's gun," Carl said. "Only fingerprints on it are yours, Molly. It was cold—I wore gloves that night, remember? I hung on to the gun—it's all wrapped up and put away safe. So I've got proof. All you've got is a story, your word against mine."

"You ran away that night," she flared. "That's proof."

"My mother never reported the truck missing," Carl said. "So nobody knows when I left. Forget it, Molly. Get out of here and leave me alone. If you come pestering me, it will be me that tells the sheriff. You worked for old man Dowd, not me. You knew about the money. You were the one had your eye on it. You were the one killed him to get it."

"I want my half," she repeated stubbornly. "You wouldn't dare tell. You'd lose all of this."

"This wasn't bought with old man Dowd's money, for Christ's sake," he said. "I couldn't have bought a used car with what was in that fishing-tackle box."

Molly frowned. "Then where—?"

"I used it to gamble with," he said. "In Las Vegas. Faro, poker, blackjack, dice. I was stupid and I lost damn near every penny. I was worse off than here—had to sleep in the truck, live on potato chips. Finally I figured even the egg ranch was better than starving. So I headed for home."

"You didn't get home, Carl, it's been years."

"I had twenty bucks in my shoe, and I stopped at Santa Anita. I hit a Pick Nine. You know what that is? You manage to pick the winners in all the races and they practically give you the damn racetrack. For a sixteen-dollar bet."

"But where have you been?"

"Found a partner, a lawyer. He had the brains, I had the money. I bought a broken-down tavern in Azusa, fixed it up, got it going again. Sold it for twice what I put into it and did the same with another in Pasadena. Then I was ready to come home like any man wants to come home." He turned and pointed at a big glossy car. "Mercedes. Forty thousand dollars, Molly." He glanced around again to be sure they were alone. "Not Mr. Dowd's money, not your money. Mine. Now clear out of here." He yanked her up off the chair, turned her, and pushed her back. "Back way, through the hills, so nobody sees you."

She stumbled, and had to clutch the latticework to keep from falling. She glared at him. "You'll be sorry."

"You can't tell the sheriff about me," he said.

"I can kill you, Carl." She was amazed at the sound of the words in her own ears. "Just like I killed Mr. Dowd. I can and I will. You got your money and your freedom, now I want mine. I want my half," she repeated again. "You promised. Don't make me wait."

"Get lost," he said, strode back into the building, and slammed the door.

Her father died. She found him slumped in the chair with the television going, whiskey bottle and glass on the carpet beside the chair, where so many others had left rings she'd never managed to scrub out. There was a wide stain where he'd spilled the glass this time. She worried more about how she was going to clean it up than about losing him. He'd been a torment and a burden to her for years. She wouldn't miss him. She was glad to watch him buried in the cemetery plot under the live oak beside her mother.

Then she learned she had to move. The house wasn't hers. Her father had, unknown to her, transferred ownership to his brother in Montana when he couldn't make the mortgage payments, and the brother had allowed him to live on here till he died. But the brother was dead, too, and the bank in Missoula that held the house under the agreement now was free to sell it, and that was what it did. Which was how Molly ended up in these little rooms.

All the same, her father's death eased things for her. There was only one mouth to feed, and no whiskey to buy. She quit waitressing at Snyder's. After cleaning up the units at the Gobineaus, she could come home, lie on her bed, watch TV —and think about killing Carl.

She is still thinking about it when knuckles rattle the screen door. A shadow lies on the screen. A man's shadow. The sheriff? In a panic, she crumples up the paper she's written on and jams it into the overflowing wastebasket under the sink. The blank paper and pencil she hides in a drawer. She forgets all about the gun. She's in a daze. She goes to the door, stands, hand on the latch, breathless. "Who is it? What do you want?"

"It's me, Molly," the shadow says, "Hugh Henderson."

She can't believe it. "I'm—sorry your mother died," she stammers. "I'll come—to the funeral—if you want."

"It's not about that," Hugh says. "Can I come in?"

"I'm sorry." Flustered, Molly pushes the door open. Hugh surprises her. Except for those soft brown eyes of his, he's changed from the runty boy he was in school. He's almost six feet tall, broad-shouldered, nothing frail about him. He looks handsome in a suit and shirt and tie and polished shoes. "Come in," she says.

"Thank you." He glances around at the small place. "Are you all right, Molly? Mom wrote me your father died."

She goes to the fridge. "Hot day. You want a Coke?"

"Yes, thanks. Shall I sit here?"

"Help yourself." She closes the refrigerator, sets a can in front of him, sits down, and pops the top of her can. "I've got a job at the Sleep EZ motel. I get along."

"My mom wrote me about that." He opens his own Coke. "It's why I checked in there last night. I thought I'd see you. I wanted to talk to you."

Molly's heart begins to hurry. "To me? What about?"

He shrugs, smiles, opens his hands. "My mom kept me up to date with everything going on in Poinsettia. She never got it through her head I hated the place, just wanted to forget it." He laughs bleakly, shakes his head. "And now she's dead. And I'm going to miss those letters." He looks at her with tears in his eyes. "Crazy, isn't it?"

Molly smiles bitterly. "I even miss my father—and you know what he was."

Hugh nods sympathetically, but his mind is back on his reason for coming here. "Mom wrote me when somebody robbed and shot Mr. Dowd. She said the sheriff questioned you about it."

"Only 'cause I worked for him," Molly says. She shrugs. "It was a long time ago."

"Same time Carl Wynant left town," Hugh says. "His mom told my mom about it—she was hurt enough Carl left, but what really burned her was he took the truck." Hugh drinks some of his Coke, holds the can for her to see, says, "Thank you." He sets the can down and frowns. "What do you think? I think it was Carl that robbed Mr. Dowd. He was always telling me the old man hid money in his house." Hugh glances at her wryly, and away again. "Back when we were friends. Carl wanted to escape from Poinsettia, that egg ranch. To live like people—that's how he put it. What good was the money to Mr. Dowd, anyway, sick as he was, dying?"

"Carl's back," she says. "He owns the roadhouse now."

"I know." Hugh draws a breath. His gentle brown eyes find Molly's, and hold them, grave, insistent. "After he did what he did to me, Mom wrote she'd see you and Carl together driving past in the truck, on your way out of town. But not toward Wynant's ranch. On the way to Copenhagen, right?"

"How do you know about Copenhagen?"

Poker-faced, Hugh says, "He used to take me there, too."

Molly opens her mouth, but she can't find words.

Hugh says, "Mom figured you two were sweethearts."

Molly blushes. "You know how this town gossips."

"Come on, Molly. He told you about the money at Dowd's, too, didn't he? That was a plan he had. To have sex with you, make you think he loved you so you'd let him in with your key and show him where the money was hidden.''

Molly jumps up. "You're lying. Get out of here."

But he only sits looking at her quietly with those gentle eyes. She struggles to get her breath, to stop trembling, to find her voice. She shuts her eyes and nods in defeat. "He did that. That's just what he did." She sits down again. "He said he loved me and after we got Mr. Dowd's money we'd go away together."

"A real sweetheart," Hugh says. "He always was."

"I wish he was dead."

"That what the rifle's for?" Hugh reaches for it from his chair, lays it on the table. "Is it ready to shoot?"

"My father taught me how to clean it, oil it, load it," Molly says. "Yes. It's ready to shoot."

Hugh stands and closes the door. "Let's talk," he says.

It's a good night. A full moon shines on the smooth, round dry-grass hills outside town. Hugh has a beautiful new car. It smells of newness. It purrs almost soundlessly along the highway, and when Hugh swings it onto the two-lane country road that leads to Copenhagen it scarcely notices the ruts and potholes in the neglected tarmac. Molly sits with the rifle between her knees. Her hand keeps stroking the velvety upholstery of the seat. She is so happy to be riding in this lovely car, she forgets for long minutes at a time where they are bound for and why.

In the dim glow of the elaborate instrument panel, Hugh's face is set grimly. When she glances at him, it reminds her, and she takes her hands from the softness of the upholstery and puts them on the cold wood and steel of the gun. This is the night she has been waiting for all these years. She looks out at the moonlit hills, the shadows of the scattered oaks on the hills, stars above, a far-off ranch house, lights aglow. It's beautiful. Her heart swells at the beauty of it. She turns suddenly to Hugh. And he is beautiful, too. She wants to lean across and kiss him.

He glances at her. "You all right?"

She catches hold of herself, nods stiffly. "Fine."

He reads his watch. "I hope he's not early." He switches off the headlights and slows the car to a crawl. She can see why. There, to the far left, the great deserted barn that is Copenhagen looms up, the moon silvering its roof. Hugh glances into the rearview mirror. There is a mirror on Molly's door. She looks into it. The road lies dark behind them. Hugh spins the steering wheel and gingerly eases the car, bumping, between the crooked fenceposts that long ago shed their gate and up the two-rut road toward the barn. It is so still she can hear the tall weeds brush the underside of the car.

"Get the gun ready," Hugh whispers.

She lifts the rifle. The space is too cramped. She hears a soft whine, and the window beside her opens. She jacks a bullet into the chamber, pokes the barrel out the window, and works an arm out to balance it, her head out into the cool night to lay a cheekbone against the stock. The hardpan of the yard is rough and this jiggles the gun. But there's nothing to fire at. The yard is empty.

Hugh stops the car in the middle of the yard and switches off the engine. There is enough moonlight so when she looks at him she can see his white teeth bared in a smile. "We got here first," he says.

Molly draws in the gun, opens the door, gets out into the silence, the gun hanging in her hand. It's not like the other times she came here, is it? She felt wonderful those times. Well, she feels wonderful tonight, doesn't she? It's just a different kind of wonderful, that's all. The other was foolish. This is real. She reaches into the car and Hugh puts a flashlight into her hand.

"Good hunting," he says.

"Don't worry," she says, switches on the flashlight, and walks into the barn. It hasn't changed much. Bums have used it, so there are cans and bottles and paper trash strewn around, but she just kicks these aside in her walk to the ladder.

The loft is the same. She stands at the top of the ladder in the deep straw for a minute, wanting to go to the corner where Carl spread out the sleeping bag and they made love. A lump forms in her throat. Her eyes grow misty.

But she turns away. Over there gapes the big door used to pulley bales from trucks below up into the loft. The door looks down on the barnyard. She goes there, making the old planks creak, lays the rifle on the straw, and stretches out beside it. She turns off the flashlight and looks down on Hugh's car with the moonlight shining on it. She smiles to herself. It all seems so simple now. But she could never have done it alone. Molly Byrne could never have lured Carl out here. It took Hugh Henderson's "How are you, old buddy?" on the telephone to do that. She watches the empty road.

She reads her watch. It is still not nine o'clock. Time is standing still. What if he doesn't come? What if he sensed Hugh was lying when Hugh told him he had brought home with him naked, grinning photographs of the teenage Carl doing obscene stuff for Hugh's camera in his bedroom out at the egg ranch and Hugh wanted ten thousand dollars or he'd show them to the Poinsettia newspaper? Hugh told Molly it wasn't true. The pictures once existed, all right, but the day he left Poinsettia he angrily burned every picture he'd ever taken of Carl, and all the negatives. He was smooth and menacing on the phone, but is Carl really so stupid as to come alone to this godforsaken place to meet a man who hates him as Hugh Henderson does? Along the road, the shadows of the trees shift as the moon climbs higher in the sky.

Her watch says it is now ten past nine. Hugh has gotten out of the car and stands leaning against it, arms crossed, gazing toward the road.

"He's not coming!" Molly calls.

"Be quiet," he says, without looking up.

And soon, light flickers beyond the farthest hills. Moving light. The lights of a car. She keeps her gaze on them. They vanish and reappear, each time closer. Then the car is within sight. It comes on, following the beams of its headlights.

It swings in at the entrance to Copenhagen. It is the sleek Mercedes. Its headlights jitter a little over the uneven ground of the yard. Molly turns, picks up the rifle, fits it against her shoulder as her father taught her, and squints, sighting along the moonlight-glinting barrel. The car rocks to a halt and the sound of its engine dies in the night silence.

Hugh takes a step toward it. The headlights of the Mercedes shut off and the door opens. Carl, dressed in white, climbs out. Hugh walks toward him. He reaches into his jacket pocket and takes out an envelope. It's nothing but a piece of junk mail from Molly's wastebasket under the sink, coupons for laundry detergent, not photographs. He holds it out to Carl. And this is the moment, the split second she has been waiting for all these years. Her finger tightens on the trigger.

A plank creaks. The floor of the loft shakes under her. A voice behind her says, "Don't shoot, Molly." The rifle barrel wavers. The rifle fires. Below, in the moonlight, Hugh Henderson yelps, throws up his arms, spins drunkenly, and falls. That's all she sees.

Rough hands jerk her to her feet, fling the rifle aside. It's the sheriff. He must have been here all along, hiding in the shadows. Carl must have sent him. "Didn't you hear me?" He gives her an angry shake. "I told you not to shoot!"

"You spoiled my aim," she cries, "you spoiled my aim!"

McIntyre's
Donald

Around midnight, the sound of rain woke him, lashing the window glass, sluicing from the eaves. Wind bent the trees and made them creak. It interfered with his listening. For sounds from Margaret. He was going to lose her. It was only a matter of time—days, a week or two at most. So he slept lightly, though to lie awake in the dark was pointless. He could do nothing for her. Even the hospital, with all its glittering equipment, couldn't stop the inevitable. They plainly had given up when last Sunday the staff let her have her way and come home. She wanted to die at home.

She'd been through surgery twice, and chemotherapy, and feeble, fretful combat with the cheerful, no-nonsense experts sent around to help her tone up her muscles, get her to walking again, feeding herself, all that. Feeding herself? She scarcely ate anymore, a spoonful of soup, a sip of juice. To make him think she was trying. But the pain was worsening, and she wanted to die. She had not said so for fear of hurting him, careful as always of his feelings. But he knew.

He reached out, switched on the lamp, and with an old man's heavy slowness threw off the bedclothes, swung his feet to the floor, sat on the edge of the bed, sighing, putting on his glasses. He took his teeth from the bedside water tumbler, fitted them into his mouth. Ridiculous, like everything about growing old. He pushed his swollen feet into slippers, stood, took his bathrobe off the bedpost, flapped into it, and crossed the hall to look in at her.

There was a night-light. She was sleeping, breathing stertorously. That was the effect of the medication. So . . . all was as well as it would ever be. He started to turn away, heard the drip of water, and turned back. He flicked the light switch. Rain was leaking through the ceiling. Not on the bed. Not yet. But he must stop it. He got a flashlight from a kitchen drawer, struggled into the stiff old raincoat that hung by the back door for emergencies, found a pail of patching tar and a putty knife in a wooden locker on the rear deck, and went down the steps.

An aluminum ladder lay beside the carport. He dragged it to the lowest segment of the roof, stood it up, settled its legs firmly, stuffed flashlight and putty knife into coat pockets, and, tar pail in hand, began to climb, squinting up into the dark, the rain in his face making his glasses useless.

He was too old for this. Stiff. Rheumatic. Every step was a struggle. He would have done better with both hands free, but not much better. It was slow going. His heart pounded with urgency, but he knew better than to try to hurry. At his age, when you tried to hurry you only made mistakes. And he mustn't fall. What would become of Margaret then?

His head came above the roofline. He was getting there. He drew a deep breath and took another step. Right leg. Left leg—the one that sometimes gave out on him without warning. The roof was at chest level. Another step. Now he could crawl onto the roof. He set the pail there. He brought his left leg up and pushed with the right, because it was the strongest.

But nothing happened. He'd grown too heavy, hadn't he? He'd have to climb higher on the ladder. And step out onto the roof. Grunting, he climbed higher on the ladder. How cold rain-wet metal felt to the hands! Now, then, he had to calculate how to get off the ladder onto the roof. To step off sounded fine when he said it to himself. But how to manage it? This side? That side? There was a pine branch to duck under. He leaned, put out one leg, thrust with the other, dropped onto the roof on hands and knees.

To get to his feet was a struggle, but he managed it. Picking up the tar pail, he climbed to the place where he knew the leak originated—a join in the roof that had given the same trouble before. He shone the flashlight on the place, knelt, pried open the pail, and smeared on the tar with the putty knife. He took out the flashlight again to inspect his work, added more tar, resealed the pail, and one small, cautious step at a time, made his way back down the wet slope to the ladder. He set the tar pail at the roof's edge, gripped again the cold metal of the ladder, and put out a leg, groping with his foot for a rung. He found the rung all right, but his leg wouldn't hold him. And he fell.

He was in his bed. It was still night, still raining. He should have been soaking, but he was dry, and in dry pajamas, and the bedclothes lay over him neatly. He switched on the lamp. His teeth leaned in the water glass. His bifocals lay folded beside the glass. What the hell had happened? He'd fallen off the roof. Crazy old fool. He tested fingers, arms, legs. All seemed in working order. His head ached. He touched his skull. Tender at the back. Painful. But how had he got here? He started to struggle up. He was bruised, all right, bruised all over. With a groan he lay back down.

And the door opened. A young man in a black leather jacket looked in, then stepped inside, a strapping young man with a round face, thick dark eyebrows, and blue eyes. For a split second McIntyre thought he ought to know him. The young man said, "You're awake. Good. I was afraid you might be in a coma. I thought about calling an ambulance, but I couldn't find any broken bones. There could be internal injuries, though. You tell me."

"Just bruises." McIntyre peered. "I climbed up to patch the roof. It was leaking. Did I do it?"

A nod. "You did it. What's wrong?"

McIntyre was struggling to get up. "Across the hall. I want to see if the dripping's stopped. My wife—"

"I checked," the young man said. "It's stopped."

"Is she all right?"

"She's sleeping."

McIntyre felt lost. "Who are you? Where did you come from? It's the middle of the night."

"I was—just getting home," the young man said. "I heard you fall."

"I appreciate it," McIntyre said.

"Can I bring you anything? Aspirin? Hot milk?"

"No, thank you."

"You want me to phone Dr. Hesseltine?"

"I'm all right," McIntyre said. "You know me—a tough old bird."

The young man was watching him steadily. As if he expected something. Not like money. Not that. Something else. Did he want to be recognized? *You know me.* Now, why had McIntyre said that? To a stranger. Only he wasn't a stranger, was he? Inside McIntyre a beautiful light went on, and "Donald," he said, before he could stop himself.

"Yes?" The young man cocked his head, half smiling, half frowning.

"I'm sorry." McIntyre groped out for his glasses, put them on. His face grew hot with embarrassment. He felt preposterous. "I mistook you for someone else."

"I guess not," the young man said. "I'm Donald."

McIntyre shut his eyes. It was his head, wasn't it? He had struck it when he fell, and he was hallucinating. He squeezed his eyelids tight and breathed in and out deeply for a count of ten and opened his eyes again, and the young man was gone. He laughed shakily to himself. *Donald.* What had made him say that? Donald was not real. He was McIntyre's private dream. His imaginary son. He had no son. He had three daughters. Used to have. Now they lived in other corners of the country. They wrote, and sometimes phoned, but rarely visited. They had husbands, and children in high school, even in college. They were busy with their own lives. He had no son. He had lived his entire long life surrounded by women, as a boy with his widowed mother and her sister and his own three sisters, then as a man with Margaret and the three girls. He had never had a son.

But the old saying was not true—you *could* miss what you never had. He'd yearned for a son, and whimsically brought a son to life. In his mind, his daydreams. Whenever it pleased him, whenever he felt the need, alone at his insurance agency, when business was slow, or since retiring, walking on the beach, say, exploring the tide rocks for shellfish, chopping out poison oak from under the pines around the house, waiting long hours at the hospital. My son Donald. A tear-away runner and climber of trees, an artful looper of scuffed basketballs through rusty hoops, a hotdog rider of spiderbikes, a surfer in long, sun-faded trunks, a glum student slouched over homework at the kitchen table, can of soda in one hand, slice of pizza in the other, a boy. Sometimes younger, sometimes older. Donald, my son.

Smiling, McIntyre slept.

He skipped his early-morning walk today. He washed and fed Margaret. He changed the bed linens, while, wrapped in a blanket against the damp and chill, she huddled in a chair by the window, where she could look out. Ordinarily at these times, she was silent. In pain. This morning she spoke. "That's the second sheriff's car that's passed," she said. "I think they're coming from Gertrude Schumwald's." But that was all. Her eyes closed. Her head drooped. His bruises made it painful to lift her—out of the bed, into the bed. He groaned, but not aloud. Thrusting needles into her pathetically wasted flesh always made him flinch inside, but he smiled and spoke gently, doing it. She murmured, smiled for him, feebly squeezed his hand, and slept again.

Now he sat in the kitchen with coffee and the newspaper,

and Henry Winston knocked on the back door and stepped inside. They'd been neighbors for years. Henry was retired, too. Used to own a drugstore in Morro Bay. Sold it to a chain outfit. It had lost all its character now. He hung up a Giants baseball cap and a windbreaker jacket. "You all right? Got a shopping list for me? Have to drive into San Luis today. Means a market with a lot more variety. Craving anything exotic?" He pulled out a chair and sat at the table. "How's Margaret?"

"No change." With a wince, McIntyre rose to get him a mug of coffee. When he set it down, he laid the list beside it. "Keeping her out of pain's about all I hope for."

"I see the ladder's up." Henry poked the list into his shirt pocket, and emptied a packet of sweetener into his coffee. "Roof leaking again, was it?"

"I patched it," McIntyre said.

"It needs to be replaced." Henry reached across for McIntyre's spoon, and rattled it in his coffee.

"Can't afford it." Henry had left the door ajar. McIntyre got up and closed it. "Hospitals, doctors."

"You've got insurance—you were in the business."

McIntyre snorted. "We'd be on the beach without it. Doesn't mean I've got thousands lying around for a new roof."

Henry shrugged. "Long as you can still climb up there."

McIntyre opened his mouth to tell Henry about his fall and what had happened afterward, but he didn't. In all his life, he had told no one about Donald. Not even Margaret. Especially not Margaret. She might have construed his daydream as a reproach to her for failing to give him a son. Were he to confide about Donald now, Henry would think he was out of his mind. Which, of course, at least last night, he had been. From concussion. But to explain away the many visitations of Donald in the past wouldn't be so easy. He could think of no excuse for those himself. "May I?" Henry picked up the newspaper and, squinting, turned over the pages noisily.

"What are you looking for?"

"Gertrude Schumwald had a break-in last night." Henry laid

the paper down. "Guess it happened too late to get in here. They print this early so they can truck it up here from L.A."

A widow, Gertrude Schumwald lived in a two-story place up at the corner, surrounded by shaggy old pepper trees. Most of the trees in Settlers Cove were high-reaching spindly pines, shallow-rooted, likely to blow down in storms off the sea, but fast-growing, so the place remained a community in deep woods.

"A break-in?" McIntyre said. These had become common lately. Settlers Cove had once been free of crime. Now street people drove up from Los Angeles or down from San Francisco to mug elderly walkers of dogs in the woodsy lanes, to hold up the souvenir shops in Madrone, across the highway, to invade houses and take televisions, microwaves, jewelry—whatever they could sell to buy drugs.

"Gertrude heard a noise," Henry said, "got Ernie's old revolver out of the dresser drawer, walked to the stair head in her nightgown in the dark, and shot it off."

McIntyre laughed. "That's our Gertie."

Henry grinned. "He dropped the silverware chest, dived out the window, and ran like hell."

"On the other hand," McIntyre said, "it could have got her killed. Impulsive, foolhardy. She always was that way. Did she get a look at him?"

"A glimpse. There's the corner streetlight, you know, but it's dim, and the rain made it dimmer. He was young, that's all." Henry took a swallow of coffee, remembered, shook his head. "That's not all. He left footprints in the mud. Big fella —heavy, too, the way they sank in."

"Black, of course?" McIntyre said regretfully.

"Not this time. Deputies asked Gertrude more than once, but she stuck to her story—he was white."

McIntyre woke to heavy footsteps on the front deck. A stranger, then. Only strangers came to this house that way, up the long path and wooden stairs from the trail below. Friends came by the side trail to the back door. He lay on the couch, an afghan over him, the book he'd been reading splayed open on his big belly. His glasses? He pawed around for them, found them, laid the book aside, threw off the afghan, sat up. Pains jabbed at his lower back, his joints. His head still throbbed. He struggled to his feet. Someone knocked on the door. A firm, loud knocking.

"Coming," he said hoarsely and hobbled to open the door. The day was beautiful though chilly. The sky was washed a flawless blue. Splintered sunlight fell through the pines. The man who'd knocked wore neat khaki. He was a sheriff's deputy. He pushed back his hat. "Mr. McIntyre?"

"Yes. It's Lieutenant Gerard, isn't it?"

Gerard sketched a smile, and nodded. "How are you?"

"That's quite a question to ask an old man. I could keep you here for hours listening to a catalogue of my aches and pains. What's on your mind, deputy?"

"Mrs. Schumwald was robbed last night," Gerard said. "Around midnight."

"So Henry Winston told me."

"We're busy after the storm, so I'm on my own asking neighbors if they saw or heard anything. Mrs. Schumwald scared him off with a handgun. She says he hit the ground running. He didn't run past here, by any chance, did he?"

"If you mean down the road, I wouldn't have seen him. I was out back." He pointed with a thumb over his shoulder. "I doubt if I'd have heard him, either. Storm was making too much noise. My roof started leaking, I climbed up and put tar on the leak. Then I proceeded to fall off."

Gerard frowned concern. "Oh, no. Are you all right?"

McIntyre touched his skull, wincing. "Slight concussion—I think that's the worst of it. Wasn't much of a fall. It's a low roof back there. No bones broken."

"I can run you to the hospital. You should have X rays. Best to be sure about these things."

"Thanks, I'm all right," McIntyre said.

"Well, you take it easy, now." Gerard went off across the damp deck that was strewn with pine needles and twigs the storm had brought down. "Sorry to bother you."

McIntyre said, "No bother," and closed the door.

"Aren't you going to tell him about me?" Donald said. There he was, big as life. He'd laid new logs on the fire and was poking up a blaze. He looked over his shoulder at McIntyre. What was his expression exactly? Those thick, dark eyebrows were raised. Was he smiling? The blue eyes seemed to twinkle, but McIntyre couldn't say whether they were mocking him or not.

"What are you doing here?" he said.

"You were asleep." The poker clanked against the fire basket. "I thought I'd better sit with Mother just in case. I read to her awhile. But I don't think she heard me."

"She's not your mother," McIntyre said sharply.

Donald straightened, set the poker back in place, and read his watch. "She'll need her medication in ten minutes." He left the room. "Don't forget." His voice came from the kitchen. A moment later, the back door closed.

McIntyre had never before in his life spoken a cross word to Donald. He felt a stab of remorse, and hurried to the kitchen. He snatched open the door. "Donald?" He stepped out onto the rear deck. "Please, I'm sorry." But Donald was gone. No one was in sight. Only a mule deer, a few yards off up the slope among the pines. It raised its antlered head, ears alert and twitching, looked at him for a second with large brown eyes, then bounded away, crashing through the undergrowth.

McIntyre stood on the deck, frowning to himself, wondering if the deer were real. Donald was certainly not real. Donald was a part of his mind—a maverick part, broken loose. Telling him it would soon be time for Margaret's injection. No stranger would know that. He, McIntyre, knew it, and had put the reminder to himself into Donald's mouth. *Aren't you going to tell him about me?* McIntyre had wondered for a moment there if he oughtn't to tell Gerard about Donald, and had tossed away the notion. And Donald had caught it. *Mother.* McIntyre shut the kitchen door. In Margaret's room, the book lay face down on the chair arm. *Pride and Prejudice*. He picked it up, peered at the page, but couldn't remember whether this was the place where he'd last left off reading to her himself or not.

Margaret spoke softly. She was very white against the pillows. He knew why: the morphine was wearing off.

"Something wrong?" she asked him.

"No, no. I fell asleep. Meant to come in and read to you. Would you—like me to read to you?"

She shook her head and turned it to see the small white bedside clock. "It's time for my injection."

"Of course." He laid the book down.

He was sweeping the front deck when the sound of a car in the driveway out back made him lift his head. A big, tough engine and, a moment later, the slam of a heavy door. A Cherokee. He knew those sounds, and wondered what had brought Belle Hesseltine. He leaned the broom by the door and went inside. By the time he reached the kitchen, Belle had let herself in.

A gaunt, upright old woman, in blue jeans, mackinaw, cowboy boots, she'd come to Settlers Cove years ago to retire, and had been busier doctoring here than she'd been in all her life before, or so she claimed. The fact seemed to be, she had no idea how to retire. Doctoring was what she'd always lived for. A love and compassion for people that she tried to hide behind a gruff manner wouldn't let her stop helping them. She hung up her Stetson. Her medical kit was in her hand.

"Sit down, Raymond. Sheriff Gerard is worried about you. He rang me to say you had a bad fall last night." She pulled out a chair at the table. "Concussion, he said, and you wouldn't let him take you to the hospital. Come on, sit down. Let me look at your head."

"What's wrong with my head," McIntyre said, "is inside. Nothing you can see. Forgetting names. Losing things."

"That's just old age." She pushed him down on the chair, set the kit on the table among the breakfast dishes he hadn't yet cleared away—he hadn't felt up to it earlier. She bent him forward, parted the hair at the back of his skull, gently touched the place he'd banged in his fall. She straightened him, removed his glasses, laid them with a click on the tabletop. She tilted up his chin, bent, and looked hard and closely into his eyes.

"How's your vision?" she asked. "Seeing double?"

He almost said he was seeing what wasn't there, but he bit that back. "No. Vision's about as good as usual—which isn't saying much."

"You've had these ten years." She handed him back the glasses. "Time you got fitted with new ones."

"Can you talk to Margaret a few minutes?" McIntyre put the glasses on. "You're one of her favorites. Not many people come anymore."

"A good many that would if they could," Belle said wryly, "are dead and gone."

"I know." McIntyre rose with a sigh. "But I can't say it to her anymore." He gathered up the dishes from the table and set them in the sink. "It sticks in my throat."

"I almost didn't make it myself." Belle took up her kit. "Big black-tailed buck cut across the road right in front of me. I didn't hit him. I braked, but the road's wet and slippery. I damn near piled up in the ditch."

"I saw him around noon," McIntyre said. "Out back here in the trees. Must be ten years since we had deer in Settlers Cove. Over across the highway, yes, but with all the building here—"

"There's been bears reported," Belle said, and headed for the hallway. "Haven't been bears on the central coast in a century. I wonder if our four-footed friends are trying to tell us something."

McIntyre laughed briefly, and began to run hot water into the sink. He poured detergent into the stream of the water. Fumbled for the dish mop. Began to wash the breakfast dishes. He rinsed each plate, mug, glass, under the running hot water and set it in a rubber-coated wire rack on the counter. He moved slowly, and winced at the ache of his bruises. He must have groaned aloud. He did that sometimes in his weariness these days, more often than he should, because there was no one to hear. But at this moment there was. Belle had not left the kitchen. She'd stood watching him, and now she touched his arm.

"Raymond, where are those girls of yours? Why aren't they here, looking after their mother? You're not up to it. Seventy-six years old. All on your own."

"I manage," McIntyre said stiffly.

"Have you written them? Have you telephoned?"

"They've got husbands, children, jobs to look after. And they're none of them nurses. What could they do that I can't do? Besides"—annoyingly, tears came to his eyes, his voice wobbled, and he turned away—"it won't be much longer." He pulled a paper towel off the rack, dried his eyes, blew his nose. "For them to come all this way . . ."

"It's their mother who's dying, for God's sake," Belle said. "Aren't you even going to give them a chance to show they love their mother?"

McIntyre shook his head. "Emotional blackmail? That's not our style, Belle—not Margaret's, not mine."

Belle snorted again. "Raymond, what ails you is pride. You don't want anyone able to say you failed in your duty. You'll carry all the weight yourself if it kills you."

"Margaret will be waiting for you," McIntyre said. "She knows the sound of your car."

Belle sighed, studied him a moment, then with a grim shake of her head went off down the hall. By the time the dishes were dried and put away, the effort had drained him. He sat down heavily at the table to catch his breath. The table felt sticky. He looked at it—splotches, smears. And then at the floor, the counters, the stove. Everything was dingy, soiled, neglected. No wonder Belle felt he wasn't up to the task he'd assigned himself.

Well, it wasn't true. He'd been lazy, self-indulgent. Thrusting out his jaw, he pushed to his feet and shuffled out to get the plastic bucket, mop, sponges, scrub brush, soap, bleach. He'd make the place shine. He was coming in with his hands full when Belle entered the kitchen from the hall, carrying her kit. She studied him and his janitor's gear sardonically for a moment, and said, "I'd call a cleaning service, Raymond. Don't do this."

"Cleaning service, hell," he said. "Waste of good money. Nothing to mopping up a kitchen."

"Youth and strength," she said. "Raymond, no one keeps those forever." She took down her hat from the rack. "Growing old is nothing to be ashamed of." She went out into the sunlight of the deck and turned back. "One thing. Keep a written record when it comes to the morphine, will you? If I hadn't stopped by, Margaret would have been in a bad way. You were down to the last three cc's."

He scowled. "No. Really? I was sure I had—"

"I replenished the supply from my kit," Belle said.

"Thank you," he said, bewildered. He seemed to see in his memory's eye three of the now all-too-familiar clear, bulbous vials lined up on the medicine chest shelf. But his memory's eyesight, it seemed, was no more to be trusted now than was his actual vision, blurred, mistaking what he thought he saw for what he saw. "I'll try to keep better track," he mumbled, and poured soap powder and bleach into the dusty bucket and ran hot water into it. The mop, which had hung in the locker on the deck, was dusty, and a spider ran out of it just as he was about to plunge it into the water. He stood watching the spider scurry under the cabinet doors beneath the sink. And Belle Hesseltine was back. She stepped inside and held something up in her thin fingers. It glinted in the sunlight.

"I think you ought to look at this," she said.

McIntyre leaned the mop against the counter and went to do as she asked. It was a silver spoon. Muddy, but until it had fallen into the mud, polished to a fine gleam. Sterling. Heavy. An ornate, old-fashioned pattern. He rinsed it under the tap, dried it, and stood turning it over in his fingers, examining it. He frowned.

"Where did you find it?"

"Lying at the foot of your ladder out here. Doesn't belong to you. Not with the initial S."

"Gertrude Schumwald?" McIntyre said.

Belle said, "I'm told she had a burglary last night."

"Well, how did it get here?" McIntyre asked.

But he knew, and the knowledge made him sick.

He blinked awake. The light outside was slanting from the west and turning ruddy. He had called the sheriff's substation in Madrone as soon as Belle Hesseltine had left. To report the spoon. He was too bruised to walk over to Schumwald's. Anyway, it was the correct thing to give the evidence to a law officer. But Gerard wasn't in. McIntyre left his name, then went back to the kitchen. He began mopping the floor, but grew tired before he'd finished, winded, achy, his heart pounding, and the back of his skull throbbing again. Henry Winston arrived with white plastic sacks from the supermarket in San Luis, and when McIntyre had written Henry a check, and put the groceries away, he went and lay down on the couch. And fell asleep. Now he wheezed to his feet and went to tackle the kitchen once more.

But he was too late. It gleamed in the red sunlight, every surface spotless, floor, stove, refrigerator shiny, cabinets as free of hand smears as if new. Donald stood on the top of the little aluminum step stool, wiping down the last of the cupboards. He grinned at the gaping McIntyre.

"Pass muster?" he asked.

McIntyre said stupidly, "What are you doing here?"

"I live here," Donald said cheerfully, "don't I?" He climbed down the ladder, took the sponge to the sink, and rinsed it under the tap. "Haven't I always lived here?"

Far more quickly than usual these days, McIntyre's head

cleared. Maybe anger cleared it. "Never," he said. The spoon was in the pocket of his shirt. He flung it on the table. "You're a thief. You robbed Mrs. Schumwald up at the corner last night. You were running away when you stumbled on me out here." He jerked his head to indicate the place of his fall. "You stopped to help me, and that dropped out your pocket."

"I'll put these things away," Donald said, and began gathering up the cleaning stuff.

"I can do it, thanks," McIntyre said. "You've done enough."

"Youth and strength," Donald said with a smile, and went out with the mop, wrung dry and white, the bucket loaded with sponges, bleach, soap box, scrub brush.

McIntyre cried, "No, wait." He mustn't leave. He must be here when the sheriff came. McIntyre looked frantically down the hall, as if Gerard might have materialized in the front room. He took a step—he'd phone him again quickly. He stopped and shook his head in disgust. What good would that do? "Donald, wait." He hobbled across the kitchen and out onto the deck. But the locker doors were shut, and Donald was gone. "Donald?" he shouted. Into emptiness. There was only the wind in the pines, and from far off down the hill the crash of surf among the rocks.

Gerard touched his hat. "Sorry to have taken so long. Like I said before, the storm got us a lot of auto accidents, downed trees and power lines, runaway horses. Busy day. What's this about Mrs. Schumwald's spoon?"

"Yes. Come in. Sit down. Get you anything?"

Gerard stepped inside, took off his hat. "Thank you, that's all right. I'll head home soon for supper."

"This is the spoon." McIntyre gave it to him. "Belle Hesseltine found it this noon, out in back. At the foot of the ladder I put up last night to fix a leak in the roof. Around midnight."

"It's certainly clean," Gerard said.

"It was covered with mud. I washed it."

"Damn." Gerard rubbed a hand down over his face and blew out air. "That's no way to treat evidence, Mr. McIntyre. It could have had the thief's fingerprints on it."

McIntyre felt his face grow red. "Of course. You're right. I'm sorry."

"Belle shouldn't have picked it up in the first place." Gerard put the spoon into his pocket. "I must have told her twenty times to leave evidence alone." He sighed and looked past McIntyre, searching the sunset room with his eyes. "All right if I change my mind? I think I could use a drink."

"Good," McIntyre said. "Sit down. I'll fetch us some bourbon." He went to the kitchen, feeling strangely elated. It was a long time since he'd sat and had a drink with a man. Henry Winston never touched the stuff. And McIntyre didn't believe in drinking alone. He dropped ice cubes into glasses, poured generously from his dusty bottle of Old Grand-Dad, and carried the drinks back to the living room almost with a spring in his step.

"Thank you," Gerard said. "All right if I smoke?"

"Go right ahead," McIntyre said. "Belle won't let me use them anymore, but I still enjoy the smell."

Gerard lit up, tasted his drink, smiled appreciatively, and lifted the glass to McIntyre. "That's good whiskey." McIntyre nodded, smiled, tasted his own drink. It hit him like a blow in the chest. Another pleasure gone off limits? What was there to recommend old age? Nothing he could think of. Gerard said, "The spoon says he ran past out in back there, but you didn't see him, didn't hear him?"

"I did. I didn't understand you, earlier."

Gerard narrowed his eyes. "Didn't understand?"

"You said the thief ran down the road. The man I saw didn't. And I had no reason to think he was a thief. I fell off the roof, knocked myself cold. Next thing I knew I was safe and dry in my own bed. A young man was here. Said he'd heard me fall. Plainly he'd carried me in out of the rain, cleaned me up, put me to bed. If I hadn't regained consciousness, he was going to call the doctor."

Gerard stared. "A young man? What sort?"

McIntyre shifted in his chair. "White, six feet, late twenties, dark hair, blue eyes, hefty. Maybe he'd had some medical experience. He seemed to know I hadn't broken anything, that all that was wrong with me was a concussion."

Gerard said, "You should have told me this right off."

"I didn't connect him with the robbery," McIntyre said, shading the truth, wanting to believe in Donald, the Donald he'd created in his daydreams. There was no way his Donald could turn out to be a housebreaker. McIntyre refused to believe that. "After all, he was a good Samaritan. You don't think of someone like that as a criminal."

Gerard grunted and took another swallow of Old Grand-Dad. "You're sure you didn't come into the house on your own, get cleaned up, get into bed, without remembering it. A bad bump on the head can give people blackouts."

"You mean I imagined Donald?"

Gerard blinked. "Donald?"

"That's what he calls himself." This was like a dream. McIntyre heard himself say next, "He's been back twice today. Once, to read to my wife when I fell asleep. A second time, to clean up the kitchen for me—not an hour ago."

Gerard listened with a poker face. "Is that so?"

"Come look." McIntyre led him to the kitchen, switched on the light. "See how it shines? Well, I can tell you, it wasn't that way. It was very grubby. My wife's ill, you see, dying, and looking after her is about all I've got strength for." He grimaced. "Years do that to you."

"Looks nice." Gerard regarded the glistening surfaces thoughtfully. "And you say Donald did this for you?"

"I hate to think he was the one that stole Gertrude Schumwald's silverware," McIntyre said.

"You sure you didn't clean up the kitchen yourself?"

"Do you think I've lost my mind?" McIntyre said.

"I think you had a blow on the head." Gerard had brought along his drink and cigarette. He sat down at the table. "What did this Donald tell you about himself?"

McIntyre almost said, *He didn't have to tell me anything, I know everything about him. I invented him. Long ago. When I wanted a son for company, a son I could spend time with away from women, at ball games, hiking, sailing.* He didn't let himself say these things. Gerard was already half persuaded Raymond McIntyre was a loony. "He didn't tell me anything. Just asked how he could help."

"Why do you suppose he kept coming back?"

"He won't come back again. The second time, I knew about the spoon. I showed it to him, called him a thief."

Gerard frowned. "Risky. He could have hurt you."

"If he was that kind," McIntyre said, "why didn't he rob me? I'm old and slow. I don't keep a gun, like Gertrude Schumwald. My wife's helpless. He could have plundered this house —instead all he did was help me."

"Right." Gerard finished off his whiskey, put out his cigarette, rose. "Describe him again, will you?"

McIntyre obliged and added the black leather jacket.

"I'm going to send somebody here to take fingerprints." Gerard went to pick up his hat. As he started down the steps into the trees, McIntyre remembered how quickly Donald had vanished this noon, and called to the deputy:

"Have you seen that blacktailed buck?"

"We've had reports," Gerard said. "Fish and Game will catch him, truck him back up in the canyons. Unless some trigger-happy householder around here shoots him first."

There were only two of them, but they seemed to fill the house. A towheaded, simple-looking kid named Vern and a slender dark young woman whose badge said she was T. Hodges. She had slightly buck teeth, and beautiful brown eyes. They wore the same tan uniforms as Gerard, the same hats, and they were everywhere with their dusting powder, brushes, cellotape, blank white cards, ballpoint pens. They went over the kitchen inch by inch, the locker on the rear deck, mop, bucket, soap-powder box.

While they took his own fingerprints at the kitchen table, they asked him to recall for them just where Donald had been in the house, and so they checked the fireplace poker, too, didn't they? And quietly, courteously, the copy of *Pride and Prejudice,* and the chair beside sleeping Margaret's bed where Donald would have sat to read to her. They checked the bathroom, in case Donald had turned the taps there when he'd cleaned the mud off McIntyre after his fall.

They took photographs. They brought in a vacuum cleaner to run over all the places Donald had stepped and climbed and stood. They softly carried the chair out of Margaret's room and vacuumed that, and softly carried it back. When the door of their county car slammed below on the road and they drove off, the house seemed empty and lonely. McIntyre suddenly missed the girls. His daughters. Karen, the youngest, in particular—T. Hodges had reminded him of Karen. He closed the front door slowly, thoughtfully, and started toward the telephone. But Margaret called out to him, and he went to do what he could for her instead.

They were up in Sills Canyon, away back in the mountains. The trail they'd followed had finally just petered out. Driving its twisty ruts, McIntyre had grown doubtful, but Donald had kept urging him on. He was fifteen, now, and sure of himself. He knew this place. No, he wasn't mixed up. This was the way. And now they stood side by side at a pool shaded by old oaks draped with moss, a cool, hidden place, quiet except for the buzz of insects, the soft babble of Sills Creek as it washed down over boulders into the pool.

"Didn't I tell you?" Donald said. "A real trout pool."

"If you say so," McIntyre said.

"Give me the key," Donald said. "I'll get the rods."

He scrambled up the rocky, brushy slope. McIntyre gazed into the pool. And saw at its far side the clear, motionless, reflection of a mule deer, a buck, with antlers.

"Donald, come see," he called.

But right away the buck took fright and bounded off.

It was a cemetery, an old one, crowded with mossy headstones, statuary, even an occasional tomb. Where? He didn't know. He'd never been here. Out there was the ocean, slate-gray today, under a cold, gray sky. Gulls circled overhead, crying their creaking cries. A canvas awning on shiny poles sheltered a double row of metal folding chairs that faced a grave into which a casket had been lowered, a heap of hothouse flowers on its lid. The girls, their husbands, and five of their offspring whom McIntyre hardly recognized sat on the folding chairs, hands in their laps. They were dressed up, all of them. So was he, in a suit he hadn't worn in a long time. It was too tight. The white shirt he'd taken from a very old laundry wrapping strained its buttons over his belly. A bald clergyman, a folded umbrella hanging from his arm, read from a book so worn some of its leaves were loose. In the King James English McIntyre had requested. Margaret loved that language, and when she still had her vitality used to rail against the modernizing of the *Book of Common Prayer*. At "dust to dust," McIntyre stooped stiffly, picked up a handful of earth, dropped it onto the flowers below, and straightened, to find Donald beside him. He, too, was dressed up. He smiled, and said, "Don't worry. You won't be alone. I'll always be here." McIntyre awoke and, heart pounding, stumbled purblind and toothless across the hall. Margaret was there, drugged asleep, but there. He almost wept with relief.

When he came back from his sunrise walk, Donald was at the stove. His black leather jacket hung by the door. He'd tied on McIntyre's apron over a plaid shirt and jeans. The kitchen smelled of perking coffee and frying bacon.

McIntyre stopped in the doorway. Disbelieving. Angry. Afraid. "What are you doing here?"

"Cooking your breakfast." Donald nodded toward the hall. "By the time you're finished with Mother, it will all be ready."

"The sheriff is after you," McIntyre said.

"She's been calling for you. Wait, here's her cereal."

Carrying the warm bowl of Cream of Wheat along the hall, McIntyre paused and put a hand on the telephone, but Margaret called out again, sounding panicky, and he went to her. He went through the gentle rituals. There was no need to change the sheets this morning, thank God, and that shortened the time a little. But impossibly he'd got mixed up about the morphine again. He couldn't imagine how or why, but there was only one vial in the medicine chest. His hand trembled as he gave Margaret the injection. He broke into a cold sweat as he hurried back to the kitchen with the cereal Margaret had barely touched, however much he'd coaxed her. Henry Winston looked at him from his place at the table.

"Where's Donald?" McIntyre set the bowl in the sink.

"You're white as a sheet," Henry said. "What's wrong?"

"How long ago did he leave?" McIntyre cried.

Alarmed, Henry stood up and pulled out a chair. "You'd better sit down. Nobody left. Nobody was here."

McIntyre looked wildly at the stove. A saucepan, two skillets. And through the oven's glass pane, he saw inside eggs, bacon, and toast on a plate. A mug of coffee steamed in front of Henry. One stood at McIntyre's place as well. He yanked open the door, stepped out on the deck. "Donald!"

Henry called, "What the hell's the matter with you?"

"You sure you didn't see a young man?"

"I told you—there was no one to see."

"He was cooking breakfast"—McIntyre came inside again and closed the door—"when I got back from my walk." He took the warm plate from the oven. "See here? And where do you think your coffee came from?"

Henry tilted his head. "The pot—like every morning."

"No," McIntyre said. "I mean, yes, but Donald made it." He banged the plate down on the table. "Donald made my breakfast while I looked after Margaret."

Henry eyed him, worried, rubbing his white beard stubble. It was a privilege of retirement that a man didn't have to shave every morning of his life. Sometimes Henry indulged it for days running. "Donald?" he said.

"The one who rescued me when I fell off the roof," McIntyre said crossly. "The one who cleaned up this kitchen yesterday. I guess you didn't notice how it shines?"

"Fell off the roof? When was that? Look at you. You're shaking. Sit down here now, and eat."

McIntyre turned away. "I have to phone the sheriff."

"Will you make sense? The sheriff? What for?"

"It was Donald who stole Gertrude Schumwald's silver."

"Well, give Belle Hesseltine a call, while you're at it," Henry said. "Trying to do everything alone here, cook, housekeeper, nurse—the strain is affecting your mind. Raymond, nobody was in this kitchen. You made the coffee and cooked like always. You just forgot."

"Matter of fact," McIntyre said, "I'll call Belle first. You eat that breakfast. I'm not hungry." And he went to the phone and punched out the familiar number. Belle answered from her car. McIntyre could hear the engine. He asked, "About the morphine. You told me you'd replenished Margaret's supply. Are you sure?"

"I set them on the usual shelf in your bathroom cabinet. What's the matter?"

"How many?" McIntyre asked.

"Three," she said.

"There's only one this morning," McIntyre said.

"Call the sheriff," she said. "Don't waste any time."

"You call him," McIntyre said. "He'll believe you. He thinks that bump on the head scrambled my brains."

• •

Gerard came to the back door this time. Henry was still present. McIntyre had hinted to him to leave, but his old neighbor was plainly worried about him and didn't think he ought to be alone. Left alone, McIntyre imagined things. Gerard sat with a mug of coffee at the kitchen table now and smoked a cigarette and listened without comment or even facial expression while McIntyre recited his story again. He followed McIntyre to the bathroom to look at the lone vial of morphine on the shelf there.

"So now we know why he keeps coming back," he said, and closed the mirrored cabinet door.

"Now we know," McIntyre said bleakly. "To get his hands on drugs."

"Urban scum." Henry had tagged along and stood in the hall. "They're all the same."

"Not exactly." Gerard left the bathroom. McIntyre and Henry followed him back to the kitchen. "His fingerprints tell us he used to be an orderly at the hospital in San Luis. He stole from the supplies there. They fired him without pressing charges." Gerard poured himself more coffee and sat down again at the table. "Everybody liked him and felt sorry for him." He lit a cigarette and made a face. "They ought to have had him arrested and charged, tried and locked up. He's been all over the area thieving to feed his habit." The deputy looked glumly at McIntyre. "You were the best break he ran into yet. No middle man."

McIntyre said, "The hospital. That's how he knew about Margaret's medication. That's where I'd seen him, isn't it? And he'd seen me. Funny thing—when I came to, after I fell off the roof, I thought I knew him. But not from where."

"Don't suppose he was wearing an orderly's outfit," Henry said, "was he? Clothes change a man."

"I thought he was—" McIntyre began, and stopped.

Gerard cocked an eyebrow. "Yes?"

"Nobody," McIntyre said, and added lamely, "someone I— used to know. As a—as a boy."

"He grew up in Seattle," Gerard said. "Alan Donald Abbott. Wanted to be a doctor. Flunked out."

"They say everybody has a look-alike," Henry said. "Someplace in the world. An identical twin."

"Is there any chance you'll catch him?" McIntyre asked.

"Unless he leaves the neighborhood," Gerard said. "Yes. When desperation drives people, they trip up." He snubbed out his cigarette and got to his feet. "Thanks for calling me. Appreciate your help." He opened the door, started out, and turned back. "I'm posting officers to watch this house, Mr. McIntyre. Abbott seems to regard it as home." Putting on his hat, he moved off across the deck. "All the same, I'd lock up at night, if I were you."

Supper and the hour after supper were the best times. He read to her by lamplight, or they watched television. Then she was tired. (He sensed often these days that she was tired well before she said so, and concealed it from him, aware of how he cherished their time together, and of how little time was left them in this life.) He set aside her extra pillows, gave her morphine, drew up the bedclothes, and she smiled and pressed his hand, and slept.

He tiptoed out, and went to lock the doors. Not possible. The lock on the front door was corroded in place, the spring lock on the kitchen door was clotted with coats of old enamel. How long had it been since they'd locked this house? Had they ever done so? He doubted it. There'd been no dangers to lock out in Settlers Cove. Not then.

He put on a jacket, took the flashlight, and went out. Across the front deck, down the steps to the trail. A patrol car sat there in the dark. It was dimly lit inside. Plainly, Gerard had meant Donald to see he'd posted guards to watch the house. Probably there was another car up the side trail. Vern, the towheaded boy, sat in this car. He blinked in the flashlight's beam.

"Mr. McIntyre?" He sat up quickly and squinted out. "Anything wrong?" He reached to open the car door.

"No, no," McIntyre said. "I just came out to tell you, my door locks don't work. Lieutenant Gerard asked me to lock up, but I can't. Haven't turned those locks in years."

"That right?" Vern said. "Well, it's okay. Don't worry. We'll keep an eye on things."

"I don't think he'll come back, anyway," McIntyre said.

"Best to be on the safe side," Vern said.

McIntyre looked into the darkness of the pines. "Is there another car?"

"Up at the rear," Vern said. "Lundquist."

McIntyre started off. "I'd better tell him."

"Save yourself a walk," Vern said. "I'll tell him on the walkie-talkie."

Now came the time of day he liked least of all, when he sat alone in the kitchen, waiting for his mind's weariness to catch up to the weariness of his body. He tried to concentrate on a book, or on *Newsweek* or *Natural History*, classical music from the college station faint from a small radio on the counter. He used to make himself cocoa to help summon sleep. But lately someone—had it been Gertrude Schumwald?—had told him chicken was the best of all nature's soporifics. So he'd had Henry Winston fetch him cans of chicken broth and, when he didn't forget, he heated up and drank chicken broth. He guessed it helped. He didn't dare sleep deeply, anyway—he had to keep an ear out for Margaret.

Now he was sipping at the soup, leafing over an article about Kodiak bears, looking at the pictures, when noises on the rear deck made him raise his head. There, at the window, stood the mule deer buck, peering in curiously, eyes wide, big ears poised. McIntyre was too startled to move, and he and the beautiful animal simply stared at each other for what seemed a long time.

Then there was a bang. Someone had fired a rifle. The deer shied. Its hoofs clattered away across the deck. McIntyre stumbled to his feet, flung himself toward the door, pulled it open. Darkness. He fumbled for the switch beside the door, and light fell across the deck. Splashes of blood. A trail of bloodstains. Someone came at a run into the light. A stocky deputy he hadn't seen before. He had drawn his pistol.

"Did you shoot?" he said.

"No. Someone out here." McIntyre's heart knocked in his chest. He couldn't get his breath. He caught the deck rail and leaned on it heavily. "Shot the blacktailed buck. Did you see the blacktailed buck?"

"No," Lundquist said. "Are you sure?"

"He was here, on the deck," McIntyre said, "looking in the window. What was the harm in that?"

"Don't look at me," Lundquist said. "I didn't do it."

Vern called out of the night, "What's going on?"

"Some son of a bitch shot that mule deer," Lundquist shouted. Someone, or maybe the deer, was crashing among the trees above the house. White-faced Vern appeared panting in the kitchen doorway. He carried a rifle. Lundquist said, "Come on. Let's get the bastard."

And the two of them charged up into the woods. McIntyre listened to them trampling around in the dark. He caught glimpses of their flashlight beams. Then he realized that now was the time for Donald to appear. No one was guarding the house. He went back indoors, took the half-empty vial from the bathroom shelf and dropped it into his pocket, got the poker from beside the fireplace, and went to sit by Margaret. He knew he wasn't worth much as a guardian. But he was the only one left.

Vern found him there, nodding in the chair. He cleared his throat. " 'Scuse me, Mr. McIntyre."

McIntyre looked up. "Did you catch him?"

"No. No sign of the deer, either." His smooth young face

showed grief and anger. "But from the way he bled on your deck, I'd say he won't make it."

"You going to stay on guard now?" McIntyre was filled with a heavy sadness. He pushed up out of the chair. "If so, I'll go to bed. The young thrive on excitement." He managed a wan smile for Vern. "It wears old people out."

"We'll keep watching," Vern said.

He woke in the dark, and knew it was no use their being out there. Donald was in the room. He could hear him breathing. Panting, rather, and whimpering. He reached out and switched on the lamp. It shone on the glass with his teeth leaning in it, and glanced brightly off the lenses of his spectacles. He put these on, and turned. Donald sat on the floor, slumped back against the closet door. His right hand was over his heart. As if to salute the flag in a sixth-grade classroom. But the hand was bloody. Blood had run down the black jacket. He was staring at McIntyre and trying to speak. McIntyre couldn't hear the words. He argued his heavy old bulk out of bed, and bent over Donald.

"I'm here," he said. "How did this happen?"

"Drugstore. In Morro Bay." The words came gasping. Donald caught McIntyre's sleeve. "Water?"

McIntyre brought water from the bathroom, knelt stiffly, and held the glass to Donald's mouth. But he was too weak to take more than a sip. He turned away his head.

"What were you doing at the drugstore?" McIntyre asked. "No, don't try to answer." He set the glass down. "I know."

"You know." Donald closed his eyes and nodded. "You always knew. Everything about me." He opened his eyes again and pleaded with his eyes. "I can't help it. You know that, too, don't you? I can't help it."

"There are police cars outside." McIntyre struggled to his feet. "They'll call an ambulance."

Donald whispered, "I didn't know that drugstore had a security guard, or I'd never have broken in." Blood leaked out of his mouth. "I'm dying. I don't want to die."

McIntyre looked down at him. "You told me I'd never be alone," he said bitterly. "At the funeral. You promised. You'd always be with me."

Donald didn't answer. His chin rested on his chest.

McIntyre went to find Vern. Vern called on the radio for Lieutenant Gerard and for an ambulance, then ran up the steps two at a time. When slow old McIntyre came in, the young officer was kneeling on the floor beside Donald. He climbed to his feet, shaking his head grimly.

"It's over. He didn't make it."

"He tried to rob a drugstore in Morro Bay."

"I know. They radioed us. He was wounded. I figured they'd catch him. I didn't want to wake you up over it." He tilted his head. "Why did he come here, Mr. McIntyre? It's a long way, the shape he was in."

McIntyre shrugged numbly. "He'd helped me. I guess he thought I'd help him."

"We'll get him out of your way," Vern said, "just as soon as we can."

"Thank you."

McIntyre went to look at Margaret.

An Excuse for
Shooting Earl

Rivera was up at the seminary on the ridge, a full-fledged priest now, secretary to the monsignor, and not always free to help out Bohannon. Old George Stubbs was suffering in his joints from the dampness of the winter, as he commonly did. At Bohannon's insistence, he lay in bed in his whitewashed plank room at the end of the long stable building, alternately dozing and cussing the pain.

So when the day's last two riders came through the gate at sundown, the job of unsaddling Seashell and Geranium, watering them, rubbing their coats down, cleaning their hoofs—this work fell to Bohannon. It had been a long day. He wanted to put his feet up and have a drink. He closed the half door of Geranium's stall, went along past the other stalls saying goodnight to the other horses, some his own, some just boarding here, and stepped out of the stable into dying daylight.

He was making wearily for the ranch house when a young man he hadn't seen before stepped in front of him. Bohannon looked past him. He'd arrived in a new car—a Sterling, so new it still had a paper license plate. He was smartly dressed, meaning everything he wore had enough cloth in it to suit up two of him. He was thin, maybe even gaunt. How old? Hard to say. Less than thirty.

He said, "Mr. Bohannon? Can I talk to you?"

Bohannon said, "I was about to have a drink. Come inside and join me." Bohannon led the way into the big, plank-walled kitchen, where shadows had taken over. He sat the boy at the kitchen table, brought out whiskey and glasses with ice in them, and sat down himself. A lamp stood in the middle of the table, but he didn't switch it on. He liked sitting here in the twilight, found it restful. "What's on your mind?" He expected, with a car like that, the kid might have money enough to own a horse and might want Bohannon to board it for him. But that wasn't it.

"You're the only private investigator in this area."

But what was he doing in this area? The frame on the Sterling's license plate named a Fresno dealer. Not exactly next door. And it was a good-sized town, bound to have a PI, more than one. Bohannon only said, "That's right."

"Do you find people?" The boy had a coughing spell then. It racked him. And it sounded awful. He sipped some whiskey, grimaced, pushed the glass away. But he stopped coughing and used a handkerchief to wipe his mouth and dry his eyes. "I mean—that's one of the things private detectives do, isn't it?"

"If they can." Bohannon lit a cigarette, watching the kid. "You understand, I only do investigations on the side, part-time. These stables keep me pretty busy."

"Oh, shit. You mean you won't help me?"

"I don't know," Bohannon said. "Who's missing?"

"A man called Earl Cartmell. Do you know who he is?"

"I used to know his father," Bohannon said. "You want to tell me your name?"

"My name isn't important." He put out a hand, and Bohannon shook it. It hadn't much life to it. No strength. "Uh—Taylor, uh—Cliff Taylor."

"What do you want with Earl Cartmell? How long has he been missing?"

"That's not important either. I just want you to find him." The boy drew a wallet from those baggy trousers of his, took money from it, and spread the money on the table. "Here's a thousand dollars." His eyes, large in his wasted face, pleaded. "Like a retainer, right? I'll give you another thousand when you locate him."

"Is it your money?" Bohannon asked.

"What do you mean?" Taylor yelped. "Of course it's my money. And, oh, yes, make a—an expense sheet. I'll pay all expenses." He was reciting from instructions, wasn't he? He ticked the details off on his fingers. "Airline tickets. Hotels. Meals. Car rentals. Earl Cartmell is a gambler. That'll probably mean looking in Laughlin, Las Vegas, Reno. Gardena—the poker parlors. Santa Anita—the racetrack."

"Suppose I find him and he doesn't want to come back with me?" Bohannon said. "I can't force him. Not unless you give me a reason. Did he commit a crime? Is there a warrant out for him? If so, you want the sheriff, not me."

"You don't have to bring him back. You don't even have to speak to him. Just phone me up and tell me where he is. I'll give you a number to call." When Bohannon said nothing to this, Taylor cracked open the wallet again. "Look—how about three thousand dollars?"

"Keep your money," Bohannon said.

Taylor looked ready to weep. "You won't do it?"

"I'm shorthanded here. One sick old man, one part-time helper. I can't travel, I can't leave the place that long."

"But you have to!" Taylor shouted in despair.

Bohannon smiled a little. "Oh, I guess not. Look"—he swept up the money like loose playing cards, tamped its edges, handed it back—"Earl Cartmell's not worth the trouble. Anyway, if he's gambling, he'll lose. He always does. Then he'll come home. You know the Cartmell ranch? That's where you'll find him."

The kid sat with the packet of bills in his hand, a hand so thin and the skin so transparent blue veins showed. His head hung. Bohannon wondered if he was crying. But he was dry-eyed when he looked up. Still, he didn't say anything.

Bohannon asked, "What do you need with Earl Cartmell? What does anybody need with him?"

The boy drew breath to speak but didn't speak. He was sweating as if he'd run a long way, and when he stood up, it was like his legs were too tired to bear him. He put the money back into the wallet, put the wallet away, and moved toward the door. Bohannon followed and pushed open the screen for him to go out. He took a few slow steps along the roofed plank walkway, then turned back. "I heard you were a kind man," he said, reproachfully. "Always helping people."

"They trust me," Bohannon said. "You don't trust me."

"I'll pay you more. How much? You name it."

Bohannon said gently, "Just tell me what it's all about." The boy only looked at him bleakly. Bohannon said, "Or don't you know? That's it, isn't it? You don't know."

Without a word, Cliff Taylor, or whatever his name was, turned and went off through the twilight. To do what? Search for Earl Cartmell himself? He looked too sick.

Bohannon had almost forgotten him when Earl's name came up again. Bohannon had got three giggly and slightly scared college girls safely aboard Ruby, Buck, and Twilight, had sent them on the dependable old mounts out the gate and up the canyon road, and was trudging back to the kitchen to catch up on his bookkeeping when he heard a car turn in at the gate and checked his stride. The faded yellow pickup truck he saw used to roll in here every week or two. And he'd felt good when he saw it. But that was past. Hubert Cartmell was dead. And this could only be that empty-headed high school girl he'd married when he was old enough to know better. After that, Cartmell had stopped coming around for rides in the canyons, card games, companionable talk over drinks. And Bohannon had seen him again only in his dying days, when Cartmell sent for him.

The yellow truck halted beside Bohannon's green one, the door opened, and as he'd feared, a young woman got out of it. It surprised him mildly that she wore jeans, a plaid shirt, boots, like a working rancher. The little he knew of her, she'd preferred flounces. Nobody thought much of her, but they'd never said anything against her looks, that trim figure, the hair that glinted gold and fell to her shoulders. She could be a TV star in Western duds, Bohannon thought. Maybe the dark glasses made him think that.

"Mr. Bohannon?" She held out a hand.

He shook the hand. "Mrs. Cartmell?"

"Ruthann, please." She looked around at the green-trimmed white buildings, the towering eucalyptus trees, the flower beds, the rail-fenced corral, and the oval of hardpan where children of all ages learned to ride, jump, barrel-race. They were learning now—Rivera was leading four little ones slowly around and around. He wasn't in black suit and turned collar: the newly minted priest was a cowboy for the day—flannel shirt, Levis, boots. Ruthann Cartmell asked, "Are you busy? I need a minute of your time."

Bohannon said, "I was just going inside for a coffee break. Why don't you join me?"

She came along, limping a little, silent, preoccupied. She didn't take off the dark glasses when Bohannon opened the screen door and ushered her into the kitchen. She kept them on when he held a chair for her at the table, brought mugs of coffee to the table, and sat down opposite her.

She said, "Hubert told me if ever I was in trouble to come to you. He said you were the finest man he'd ever known. The straightest. And the wisest."

"He was a good friend." Bohannon lit a cigarette. "I'm sorry he's gone."

She laughed ruefully. "Not as sorry as I am."

"Something wrong at the ranch?"

"There's no income," she said. "When Hubert got so sick, he sold off the cattle to pay the medical bills."

Hubert had been fifty when he married her. Then in only six or seven years had come cancer, the fast-acting kind. It was shocking to see the big, robust rancher, with his long stride, his loud, laughing voice, his youthful eagerness for living every day to the hilt, reduced in a few miserable months to a skeletal, sunken-eyed wreck, scarcely able to whisper.

"I don't know how I'm going to hang on to the place." She sipped some coffee, reached across for Bohannon's cigarettes, and took one from the pack. He lit it for her. "And I have to. I can't let it go, Mr. Bohannon. I gave Hubie my solemn word."

Bohannon winced at the nickname, but he kept quiet.

She went on, "It's the Cartmell ranch. He put his whole life into it. It's his monument."

Bohannon said, "What about a bank loan?"

She laughed bleakly. "Those silver-haired old dudes put a fatherly (I don't think) hand on my knee and croon that cattle'll only ruin me. On what I'd earn from beef, I could barely pay my running expenses. I could never repay a loan, not one big enough to get the ranch back to what it was."

"So what do they advise?"

She shrugged and blew smoke away. "That I let them put the land up for sale. To real estate developers. The central coast is the coming place. Everybody wants to live here. I'll be rich." Her laugh was sad. "Where? Why?"

"Didn't Hubert own stocks, bonds, shares?"

"Not a whole lot. Earl sold his half right off, of course. And gambled the money away."

Earl was Hubert's son by his first marriage. Hubert had been so proud to have a big, strapping son like himself, he'd let the boy run wild. Earl had inherited only his father's size and strength—he'd missed out when it came to character.

"From my half, the dividends keep food on the table, gas in the truck, and a few horses in the barn."

Bohannon said, "Life's no good without horses."

"Hubie taught me that. But now I'm faced with taxes."

"So . . . what will you do? Sell the stocks?"

She said miserably, "That's all I can do. Unless—"

Bohannon swallowed coffee and watched her with his eyebrows raised.

She took a breath and blurted, "There's a man, Jeremy Essex. He's in the music business. Promotion. He wants the ranch for a week-long summer rock festival. Like"—she wrinkled her brow—"what did they call it?"

"Woodstock?" Bohannon said.

"That's the one. Years ago."

Bohannon smiled because he couldn't help it. "Ancient history." He wondered to himself how old she was by now. Thirty? Not quite. "A Woodstock by the sea?" he said.

"Jeremy wants it halfway between L.A. and San Francisco. Monterey County won't hear of it, but our board of supervisors don't seem to mind. And the Cartmell ranch would be perfect, he says. A natural whatchacallit—amphitheater—to set up the stage in, the lights, the sound system, all the space in the world for parking. Plenty of motel rooms and restaurants in the area." She put out her cigarette. "He'd pay me ten percent of the take. And the take would be millions."

Bohannon noted that she used the promoter's first name. Young and good-looking, wasn't he? "You believe him?"

"Should I? You tell me." She took a card from her shirt pocket and held it out.

"Looks impressive," Bohannon said. "But I'd check up on him if I were you."

"Will you do it for me?" she said. "For Hubie?"

"All right." He nodded, put the card into his wallet, sat down. "What if it doesn't draw—nobody comes?"

"He can get Bruce Springsteen," she said, "the Grateful Dead, Morrissey, a whole list of stars. People will come."

He tilted his head, studying her. "So why are you here? You already know you're going to do it."

"Earl's dead set against it," she said. "He wants to sell the ranch for housing tracts."

Bohannon drank. "And neither one of you can sell it unless the other one agrees?"

"Mr. Fitzmaurice says it's a terrible will," she said. "He tried to get Hubie to set up trust funds for each of us till we're older. No way. I got half, Earl got half, and that's that." She repeated her bitter little laugh. "On his deathbed, he made Earl swear to stop gambling and whoring around, patch things up with Trish, go back to his kids. Course Earl promised. But what's that worth?"

"You can still keep him from selling off the place."

"And he'll do his damnedest to stop the rock festival."

Bohannon scratched an ear. "Maybe he's right. There was only one Woodstock. This would be a one-time thing."

"But if the money is as much as Jeremy—Mr. Essex—says, I could buy livestock again, hire hands, start the ranch over. I wouldn't need another rock festival."

Bohannon worried. "Times change. In the sixties the kids wanted to sleep naked in muddy fields, wanted to hear the music in the pouring rain, wanted to be little children forever. They're not like that anymore."

"They still go to rock concerts," she said. "I did until I married Hubie. My whole crowd did."

"I'll check out Essex, see if he's real." He reached quickly across and lifted the dark glasses from her face.

She grabbed for them. "What are you doing?"

"That's quite a shiner. Who gave it to you?"

"It was an accident," she said.

"You came for help," he said. "Let me help."

She sighed glumly. "You know Earl." She put the glasses on again. "He's not too bright. When it comes to a difference of opinion, his fists are his only argument." She stood up. "I have to go. Thanks for your help."

Bohannon stood up, too. "You'd better not go back there alone. I'll trail along and straighten him out."

"This happened three days ago. He packed up and stormed off. He had a bundle of money. God knows where he got it. But he won't come home till it's gone."

"Home from where?" Bohannon asked.

"He didn't confide in me. Why?"

"Two nights back, someone came asking me to find him."

"Probably somebody he owes money to," Ruthann said.

"A skinny kid in expensive clothes, driving a brand-new high-priced car. From Fresno. He claimed his name was Cliff Taylor. Mean anything to you?"

"Earl never talks about his friends." She smiled and laid a hand on Bohannon's arm. "I'll be all right." She headed for the door. He followed her. She limped past flower beds. "Hubie's guns are still racked up there in his den. And he taught me how to use them." She opened the pickup's cab and climbed aboard. "It would be nice to have an excuse for shooting Earl." She slammed the door, started the engine, and smiled down at Bohannon. "Now, wouldn't it?"

It was still dark when Bohannon went out to the stables to do the morning chores. By the time he'd finished, the sun had topped the eastern ridge and dew sparkled on everything—rooftops, pickup and stake trucks, horse trailers, fence rails, stretches of mowed grass. He showered, shaved, and dressed. And when he walked into the kitchen, carrying his best boots, Stubbs was at the cookstove fixing breakfast. The smells in the air were good ones of coffee, bacon, cornmeal mush frying in butter. Bohannon sat down at the table and pulled on the boots.

"You're supposed to be in bed," he said.

"So you can have women running in and out of here at all hours?" Stubbs poured coffee and brought a mug to the table for Bohannon. "What would Father say?" He meant Rivera, who was half Bohannon's age and a quarter Stubbs's.

"She's a client," Bohannon said. "Strictly business."

"Hah," Stubbs said. "That pom-pom girl Hubert Cartmell went crazy over, wasn't she?" He hobbled back to the stove. "Any reason you couldn't go crazy, too?"

"I'm not old enough," Bohannon said.

"You're getting there." Stubbs laid the fried bacon on a brown paper grocery sack to drain and set out golden-brown slices of fried mush next to them. Now he cracked eggs into the bacon grease. "What are you all dressed up about? Who'd you swipe the suit and tie from?"

"They've been in my closet." Bohannon tried the coffee. Too hot. "Can't you smell the mothballs?"

"She's sending you to the wicked city, ain't she?"

"Hollywood," Bohannon said. "The music business."

"I figured as much." Stubbs hovered over the eggs. The hand that held the spatula was warped, the joints swollen. But he managed, and he was tetchy about offers of help. "Talk is there's gonna be a big rock-and-roll thing at the Cartmell ranch, end of August."

Bohannon was surprised. "Talk is—where?"

"At the drugstore." Stubbs laid the eggs neatly on plates, sunny side up. "Seems to me I'm always in there. Pills. Capsules. Rubs. Haven't found one yet that works." He put bacon and mush on the plates and brought them to the table. "To hear the ads on the radio"—he sat down and tucked a napkin in at the neck of his shirt—"you'd think every one of them had discovered the final cure for pain at last."

"Nobody wants the final cure." Bohannon poured a lick of maple syrup on the crusty chunks of mush and picked up his fork. "Who at the drugstore, George?"

"Gawky kid that works there," Stubbs said. "Hair done up all spiky. He's all on fire about it. Rattled off a lot a names, singers and bands I never heard of. Outlandish."

Bohannon spotted Sharon Webb lined up with other earlybirds outside the bank, waiting for it to open. He liked Sharon Webb, a staunch, pug-nosed little widow, the local watchdog for the save-the-earth types, of whom there were a good many in Madrone and Settlers Cove. Retired people, mostly, keen on country living, wanting the landscape and the wildlife left as it was. They were in friendly territory. There was a seabird sanctuary not far from Morro Bay. And the Fish and Wildlife Service kept an eye out for the safety of the sea otters along this rugged coastline.

He asked her, "Have you heard about a summer rock festival at the Cartmell ranch?"

She snorted. "Earl Cartmell came to alert me soon as that nitwit stepmother of his told him. Next thing, I hear it from Celia Van Slyke, all smiles."

"Figures," Bohannon said. "She owns a motel."

"And there's twenty more like her," Sharon Webb grumbled. "And fifty Sloppy Joes, with a license to poison people with fat, cholesterol, whiskey, and gin."

"It's not a done thing," Bohannon said.

"No, and if I've got anything to say about it, it never will be. You know why I cried at Hubert's funeral? Because I could see this kind of thing coming. That trashy little—"

"She's all right," Bohannon said. "She's just trying to save the ranch."

"Save it, my foot. They'll chop up his oaks for firewood, scatter trash ten feet deep, pollute the creeks. Hack, think of the environmental impact. Otto Tylson and I are taking a delegation over to San Luis for the next supervisor's meeting, and if they won't listen, we'll go to the Coastal Commission in Sacramento. We'll get up a—"

He didn't hear what she and Otto, a wealthy real estate agent, were going to get up. The bank doors clattered open, and everybody hurried inside. Including Bohannon, who had a week's checks to deposit and, mournfully, a cashier's check to buy for Linda's care at Carlo Manfredi's place over the mountains. As to putting anything into savings, he wasn't managing that these days. Owning horses and paying for their board was a luxury some people were finding lately they couldn't afford. Business was falling off. Two years ago he'd have been able to lend Ruthann Cartmell the money to pay her taxes. This year, he'd be lucky to pay his own. He sealed the hospital check in an envelope already addressed and stamped, crossed the sleepy street to the little post office, poked the envelope through a slot, then got into the green pickup and headed south on highway 1. He had nothing to lend Hubert Carmell's widow, but maybe he could at least keep her from being swindled.

"What I'm sorry about," he told Rivera that afternoon, as he helped him muck out stalls, "is that I didn't get to see Jeremy Essex. He was out of town."

Rivera shoveled wet straw and manure into a wheelbarrow. "But the people you did see—recording executives, musicians, journalists—they assured you he is what he claims to be? He is not lying to Señora Cartmell?"

"He's not lying." With a grunt, Bohannon heaved up on the handles of the wheelbarrow and got it rolling along the passageway between the stalls. The wheel jarred over the planks. "He's put on some of the biggest concerts with some of the biggest names in the business, Elton John, Don Henley, Paul Simon, I don't know who-all. Not just in the U.S.A. Overseas. Japan. Australia. Even Russia."

Outside, Bohannon dumped the wheelbarrow and checked the sky. A few wisps of cloud to the west. Mare's tails. He judged them harmless, and he'd heard no storm warnings on the truck radio. So most of the horses out grazing on the fresh winter grass of the canyon slopes could stay the night. A few, high-strung or sneaky, he'd ride out and bring in now. It was growing late. He'd take Bearcat—the old bay gelding knew the drill.

Back in the stable, Rivera was clipping the wire bindings on a bale of fresh straw for the clean stalls. He said, "And now for his greatest triumph, this Jeremy Essex will bring rock to the central coast of California."

"Ah, but not for just one night, and not just one band." To Bearcat Bohannon murmured, "Come on, old man," opened the stall door, and led him out, hoofs thudding slow and solid on the planks. Bohannon bridled him, threw a blanket across his broad back, took down a saddle. "For a whole week, a different show with a different headliner each day."

"You don't have to sell me, Hack." Rivera's voice came from one of the box stalls, where he was laying down straw. "I will be the first in line for tickets. I will bring the entire student body from the seminary."

"Ruthann Cartmell will kiss you for that." Bohannon hoisted the saddle, but the old horse shifted ground a little, just for the hell of it, so as not to make things too easy for the man. He tossed his head and blew through his nose, pretending to be spooked. He was a great kidder.

"Stop clowning around," Bohannon told him. "This is serious business. Work to do." He put the saddle on.

Rivera said, "Will a handshake be all right?"

"Maybe for you." Bohannon bent to cinch the saddle girth. "But she'll feel she hasn't thanked you enough." He gathered an armload of lead straps and led the bay toward the bright doorway. "She may never smile again."

Rivera groaned. "I will give you the money, okay?" he called. "You buy the tickets for me."

On his way to Madrone next day, he detoured through green hills and cool canyons to have a look at the Cartmell ranch. The last leg entailed a long uphill drive between rolling pastures from the main roadway. When the ranch buildings hove into sight through their grove of oaks, he let go the breath he'd been holding, and his heartbeat slowed. Earl hadn't come home. There was no sign of the boy's beloved monster Buick convertible from the gas-guzzling years before Earl was born. Only the yellow pickup, and beside it a flashy red European sports car. Bohannon pulled his green GM up next to them, switched off the engine, jumped down, and stretched. It was quiet. Chickens clucked. In reeds down by the creek, redwings piped. He climbed porch steps and knocked. The sports car said she had company, so Ruthann ought to be stirring, but no one came.

He hiked around the sprawling house to the rear. A lone horse in the paddock swished flies with its tail. He knocked on the frame of the back door, and fat little María Cortez came waddling. "Señor Hack." She smiled and unhooked the screen door. The smile was unexpected. Back before Hubert Cartmell had married Ruthann, María had always been cheerful. Not since. She'd never desert Cartmell, but she meant to sulk until that upstart girl left this house forever.

He touched his hat brim. "Where's Mrs. Cartmell?"

"Out riding." María seemed charmed by the idea. "With that nice Englishman." She gaily waved Bohannon to the breakfast nook. "Sit down, Señor Hack. It has been a long time since you came to this house." From the stove, she brushed away whatever answer he might have tried for. "I know why, but you were wrong. And you have come back at a happy time." She brought him coffee and slices of *pan dulce,* a lemony sweet Mexican bread—the taste, wherever he met it, brought him back to this house in memory.

He was a little startled. "A happy time?"

"*Sí.* I am ashamed to say that for all these years, I did not like or trust Señora Ruthann. God forgive me, I hated her. I believed she had only married Señor Hubert for his money. What else could a young girl like that want with a man old enough to be her father? She was waiting for him to die, no? Then she would sell this rancho and go off with the money."

Bohannon buttered a slice of *pan dulce.* "You weren't the only one who believed that." He began to eat.

"Ah, but I was mistaken. When Señor Hubert died, I thought that I alone was left to defend this rancho and its memories. He had provided for me in his will, and had implored me to stay on. It was not necessary. This is my home. I have no other. It was his mother who hired me, when I was still a girl, when this house was new. I was here when he married Señora Dorothy, when Earl was born. I nursed La Vieja through her last illness, then years later Señora Dorothy, when she died so young. And last the Señor himself. Who else remained to save this rancho from the evil designs of that grasping girl?''

Bohannon drank some of María's rich coffee. "But now you know you had her wrong. We all did. She's told me. She feels the same way you do about the ranch.''

María nodded so hard two tortoiseshell combs fell out of her hair and rattled on the floor. "I know, I know." She touched her bosom. "And my heart is glad.''

"It's to raise money to pay the taxes and get some beef stock back on the place that she's going to let this man Essex put on his rock festival.''

"*Sí.*'' María bent, picked up the combs, stuck them back in place, and leaned close to Bohannon, smiling, voice low and trembling. "And do you know? I think they are in love.''

Bohannon pushed back his hat. "Is that so?''

"*Sí.* I have seen them kiss when they did not know I was nearby." Her face shadowed. "He was furious at what Señor Earl did to her. He said he could kill him for that.''

Bohannon said, "Earl brings out the best in folks.''

María was thinking her own thoughts. "She is young, and she has been alone too long. She needs a husband. And Señor Jeremy—he is very handsome. But will such a man be content to live in this—this wilderness?''

"I wouldn't count on it," Bohannon said. "But they don't have to get married for him to help her save the ranch.'' Bohannon tilted his head. "That beating Earl gave Ruthann—did you see that?''

She nodded. "Earl does not want this—this fiesta.''

"No. He wants to sell the place outright.''

"*Sí.*'' María looked grim. "This is how he respects his father's dying wish." She heaved a sigh. "I pray to the Virgin daily that this place will be spared, that I may grow old under this roof, and die in peace here when my time comes, but . . .'' She broke that off. "Anyway, you want to know what happened on Tuesday. He took from his pocket a bundle of money. Ten thousand dollars, he said. He would give it to her if she would agree to sell the ranch."

"A down payment on her half of the sale price?"

"No, no. She would still receive her entire half. He said this again and again. The ten thousand would be extra, a—a—" She waved her little fat hands. "A bonus?"

"A bribe," Bohannon said. "What did she say?"

"She asked where the money came from—it could not be his. 'What do you care?' he said, and tried to push it into her hands. She pulled away from him, shaking her head, putting her hands behind her back. She would not touch that money. When I saw how determined she was about this, I realized how I had misjudged her all these years. He followed her, shouting from room to room, and finally he struck her. This temper of his—he had it even as a child, but never like this. He knocked her down. He kicked her. I was terrified." She crossed herself quickly at the memory. "I thought he was going to kill her. I am only a woman, but I could not stand by and see this happen. I ran into Señor Hubert's den to get a gun. But when I came back, Señor Earl he had gone off and slammed the door of his room. I ran to her. She was bleeding and hardly conscious. Somehow I got her to her bed. She would not let me call a doctor. She did not want the gossip to spread. So I nursed her. I owed her this, for how coldly I have treated her all this time." She gave her head a glum shake. "You have seen only her face, but she has many bruises hidden by her clothes."

"She told me Earl packed up and left," Bohannon said. "Any idea where he went, María?"

"No." She rattled pans at the stove. "But that money was not his. So he will be found, Señor Hack. Do not worry. The one whose money it is—he will find him."

Now a ruckus started outside. Dogs barked, chickens squawked, children laughed and shrieked. A woman yelled for order. A horse neighed and Bohannon heard hoofbeats. He made for the kitchen door, slammed it behind him, ran down the back-porch steps. A pair of small dogs chased the chickens. Feathers flew. He grabbed one of the dogs up, then the second one. They wriggled happily in his arms, and licked his face. A woman came running to take the dogs and pop them through the door of a camper truck parked under an oak beside the ranch house. At the corral fence, three young kids were yelling at the panicked horse. The oldest, a yellow-haired girl in ragged jeans, was throwing stones at the horse. Bohannon ran to her, picked her up the same way he'd picked up the dogs, and turned to carry her, yelling and kicking, to her mother.

He set her on her feet. "You've got a mean one here."

Her mother slapped the girl. "Shut up, Deb."

Deb staggered backward, a hand to her face, dazed, amazed. "You hit me. You're a vicious bitch. I'll tell Daddy. He'll make you sorry."

"I'll vicious-bitch you." Her mother lunged for her.

But the skinny little girl dodged, and ran across the yard and around the corner of the barn, shrieking, "Daddy, Daddy, Daddy," all the way.

The smaller kids, two boys, Bohannon guessed, stood at the paddock fence and stared as the woman stumbled a few steps after Deb and then gave up. The youngest one, maybe four, had his thumb in his mouth. Behind them, the horse stood in a corner of the paddock, sweating, trembling. Bohannon eyed him, concluded he'd settle down by himself given time, went and took the boys by the hand, and led them to their mother.

"It's Mr. Bohannon, isn't it?" she said.

"Trish?" He scarcely knew her. She'd been a peaches-and-cream schoolgirl when he saw her married at this house eight, nine years ago. At the time, knowing Earl, he'd worried for her future. Earl was a mean, sulky nineteen when she turned up pregnant, a simple sixteen. She looked hard-bitten now, all signs of innocence vanished.

She pushed at her straw-dry, straw-color hair and tried to smile as she shook his hand. She'd lost some teeth. Earl had punched her around, hadn't he? "I guess I've changed. You haven't. You still look the same."

"I live an easy life," Bohannon said.

Her expression soured. "I don't."

"I didn't expect you would," Bohannon said. "But at a wedding, everybody hopes for the best. You here for Earl?"

"This is where he lives." She turned toward the house. "The lying bastard promised me a year's back child-support payments two weeks ago. Swore to it in a magistrate's courtroom. But has he sent the money? Hell, no." She started toward the house. "So I came to get it. That's how it always is with Earl and promises. You want him to keep them, you have to catch him first."

"He's not here," Bohannon said.

She whirled around, white-faced. "What? Where is he?"

"He took off a couple days ago. I don't know where, María doesn't know."

"What about Ruthann? Did she go with him?"

"She's out riding," Bohannon said. "Maybe she can tell you when she gets back."

" 'Out riding.' What a tough life she married into."

Bohannon saw out of the corner of his eye that Deb was coming at a drag-foot walk from behind the barn. He didn't want her tormenting the horse again. Which she might do, since her mother probably wouldn't put up with having stones thrown at her. But Deb came on without a glance at the paddock. She squinted up at her mother. "Can I have a soda?"

"Sure, honey," Trish said, hugged her, and stroked her hair. "You boys go drink a soda with Debbie."

"And leave that horse alone," Bohannon said. "Okay?"

They stared at him, as if they'd never heard a man speak before. Then they trailed off toward the Winnebago.

"They're just restless from the trip," Trish said.

"Teach them to be kind to animals," Bohannon said.

• •

He had left the ranch house out of sight behind him when he saw two riders coming up the road through the pasturelands. He pulled the pickup off into brush beside a barbed-wire fence and waited. Insects buzzed in the dry weeds. A meadowlark sang. As the riders neared, he could see that Ruthann sat her palomino gingerly, and he thought of those bruises María had mentioned. *He knocked her down. He kicked her.* Essex was in his late thirties, small and wiry, handsome and aware of it. His Levi outfit was manufactured to look worn and faded, but it was new. So were his hat and boots. The riders reined up.

"Mr. Bohannon," Ruthann said.

Bohannon jumped down from the truck. "Just passing. Stopped in to see if you were all right."

"Hack Bohannon," she said, "Jeremy Essex."

"Bohannon?" Essex scowled at Ruthann. "Hack Bohannon is a friend of yours?"

"An old family friend," she said. "Jeremy? What is it?"

"He was in L.A. yesterday, checking up on me." He glared at Bohannon. "I phoned my office—routine when I'm out of town. They told me you'd been poking around. A writer friend from *Downbeat* left word for me at my motel." He turned again to Ruthann. "I assumed he'd been hired by the Sierra Club, or the estate agents." He laughed wryly. "And now I find it was you." He shook his head. "Bit of a shock. Proves you never know people."

Ruthann looked stricken, and Bohannon lied for her. "You're wrong about that. Hubert Cartmell was one of my best friends. We went back a long way. When I heard about this proposition you'd made Ruthann, I thought I'd better be sure you were legitimate."

"And am I?" Essex said coldly.

"I'm satisfied," Bohannon said. "Don't blame Ruthann. I was the one who was out of line. Hubert never told me to watch over her, but she's young, and I didn't want her to make a mistake if I could prevent it."

Essex reached out to press Ruthann's hands, which were folded on her saddle horn. "Forgive me?" He swung down from his mount, and shook Bohannon's hand. "I've been bloody rude. Sorry. It makes me edgy to be checked up on."

"Why?" Bohannon said. "You passed inspection."

"You think like a policeman," Essex said.

"Maybe because I used to be one," Bohannon said.

"Everyone's guilty until proven innocent?"

"If some of us didn't think like that"—Bohannon climbed back into the pickup—"what would become of the innocent?" He closed the door and started the engine.

"Follow us back to the house," Ruthann called. "María's fixing lunch. There'll be more than enough."

"Thanks—I've got a lunch date in Madrone." He let go the hand brake. "Anyway, there won't be more than enough. Not this time. A crowd has arrived."

Essex had swung into the saddle, and he and Ruthann had started to ride on. She reined up the palomino. "What do you mean? What crowd?"

"Trish and the kids from hell."

"Oh, no," Ruthann wailed. "What in the world for?"

"Seems a court ordered Earl to come through with his overdue child-support payments. She's here to collect them. With blood in her eye. How can she afford a Winnebago?"

Ruthann walked the horse back to him. "That's their home—Trish's and the kids'. They live in it year round."

"You don't mean it."

She nodded. "Earl won it in a poker game. It's the only thing he ever gave her he didn't later take back."

"Where is Earl, Ruthann?" Bohannon said.

"I don't know. He had a lot of money. He could have bought a plane ticket to anywhere in the world." She frowned to herself. "When he beat me up, María screamed at him that he'd killed me. Maybe he believed her. Maybe he'll never be back." And now she smiled that wicked smile again. "Wouldn't that be nice?"

• •

T. Hodges had bowed her head and was looking at her watch when the screen door banged behind Bohannon at the luncheonette in Madrone. T. Hodges wore her deputy's uniform. She looked, as always, trim and fetching, and she gave him one of those smiles of hers that were mostly in her eyes. They were beautiful eyes, large and brown and limpid. Her smiles had a way of weakening his knees. He sat down at the gingham table and laid a gingham napkin across his knees. "Am I very late?"

"Only seven minutes," she said. "That's a record."

He told her about his stop at the Cartmell ranch. "Where would Earl Cartmell get ten thousand dollars?"

"Nobody's reported it stolen. Not to us."

"Can you check with Morro Bay and San Luis?"

"I will." Their table was on the screened porch. She peered through the main room of the eatery toward the kitchen. "Who's cooking today, do you think?"

"Not the one who burns everything," Bohannon said. "He or she only works the lunch shift one day a week."

"God pity the dinner customers," T. Hodges said.

A plump jokey young woman named Cassie took their orders. When she'd gone, Bohannon said, "What does the sheriff's department think about the rock celebration?"

"That the roads can't handle the traffic," T. Hodges said. "That telephone complaints from citizens will jam our switchboard. That car crashes will keep the highway patrol hopping around the clock. That the jail won't hold all the beer-swilling, pot-smoking, coke-snorting teenagers. That there'll be bonfires up and down the beach all night every night. That the trash cleanup will take a month and cost half the county budget." She busied herself popping the can of soda Cassie had brought, pouring from it into a glass of shaved ice. "Other than that, we think it's a wonderful idea. Lieutenant Gerard says the town council should give Ruthann Cartmell a medal for community betterment." She eyed Bohannon, who was tasting his beer. "And you're siding with her."

"She wants to hang on to the ranch," Bohannon said. "I can understand that. Hubert would be proud of her."

"Not if he knew the way she was going about it. Hack, I'm surprised. And disappointed. That little blond airhead has made a fool of you."

He shrugged. "The thing hasn't happened yet. Sharon Webb and Otto Tylson are agin it. They're on the move, and you know Sharon. She'll never give up."

"Mmm." Cassie brought bacon and avocado hamburgers for both of them. T. Hodges tilted up the bun to inspect the meat. "You were wrong," she said. "The phantom scorcher has struck again."

"Damn," Bohannon said, but he was hungry and bit into his hamburger anyway.

So did she, hopelessly. And in a minute, asked, "Don't Otto Tylson and Sharon Webb make funny allies? I know he's all for recycling, saving the ozone, and so on, but isn't what he really wants the Cartmell property? Isn't it really Earl Cartmell he's siding with, not Sharon?"

Bohannon blinked. "Maybe I'd better ask him."

"Sharon will just die if he helps her stop the rock festival, only to turn around and buy the ranch from Ruthann. In the long run, a subdivision there would do a lot more environmental damage than any rock festival."

"Sharon's heart is in the right place," Bohannon said, "but she suffers from terminal innocence."

No one was in the reception room at Otto Tylson's plush offices, but beyond the door marked PRIVATE he heard a sound that suggested somebody was here. He opened the door and looked into a big, handsome office with a picture window that gave a fine view of the mountains. No one was in here, either, but there was a side door that wasn't fully closed, and the sound was coming through that door. He said, "Excuse me," and poked his head into another room. It had been fixed up as a gym, with weights, bench, a rowing machine, and an Exercycle.

It was the whir of the Exercycle he'd heard. And Otto Tylson was pedaling it, studying a blue-backed contract as he did so.

He blinked at Bohannon, startled, then smiled a professional smile, got off the machine, laid the papers aside. He came in in white tennis shorts, a T-shirt, a towel around his neck, and shook Bohannon's hand. His eyes were intensely, almost un-really blue. His beautifully capped teeth gleamed in a crinkly smile. He was well tanned, trim in body, stood straight, moved young. But he was past fifty. Hack wondered who the realtor went to all the trouble for. Not Enid, his sensible wife, who looked her age and didn't mind it. She was heiress of an old local family, and it had been her wealth that had set Otto up in business.

"Sorry to break in on you," Bohannon said.

"Always glad to see you, Hack. What can I do for you?" Wiping his face with the towel, Tylson went to a small icebox and brought out Gatorade. He held up the green bottle. "Care for a glass? Restore those minerals?"

Bohannon shook his head. "I'll pass. I hate rattling when I walk. Reason I don't wear rowels."

Tylson laughed and poured a glass of the stuff for himself and put the bottle away. "Come in here, sit down. Let's be comfortable." Bohannon did as he was told. Tylson tilted back in a leather executive chair behind a desk heaped with work. He'd made good on his wife's investment. He never stopped. The lights often burned late here. "You aren't thinking of put-ting your place on the market at last?"

"I'm not quite broke enough," Bohannon said. "Anyway, if you buy the Cartmell ranch, that will tie up all your available funds for a while, won't it?"

"The Cartmell ranch?" Tylson's eyebrows shot up. "Some-body tell you I'm buying the Cartmell ranch? They're blowing smoke, Hack. It's not for sale. That former child bride of his is going to hang on to it if she has to ruin the whole central coast to do it. Haven't you heard about—?"

"The rock festival? I've heard about it, sure. Even met Jeremy Essex, the fellow who's going to stage it. Ruthann asked me to check up on him, see if he was legitimate. I did that. He's big-time."

Otto Tylson said, "Yes. That's what makes this thing so scary. There's money there, and power. Essex has already got the local Rotary, Kiwanis, the JCs on his side, the motel owners, the restaurateurs. We're fighting back, but show-business types like Essex can run roughshod over anything in their path—forget about who's right or wrong."

Bohannon gave him a thin smile. "Over you, Otto? I wonder. Ruthann is only part owner of that ranch. The other half is Earl's, and Earl wants to sell the place."

Tylson grew guarded. "So Sharon Webb says."

"Earl didn't tell you himself? He didn't come to you and ask your help in changing Ruthann's mind?"

"How could I help Earl Cartmell? By changing Ruthann's mind? Has she got a mind?" Now it was Tylson's turn for a wry smile. "That's news to me."

"How could you help Earl Cartmell?" Bohannon shrugged. "By helping yourself."

Tylson frowned. "What do you mean?"

"Earl turned up a couple of days ago with ten thousand dollars. It wasn't his. What his father left him, he'd gambled away months ago."

"I know that. Everybody knows that. Turned up with ten thousand dollars where?"

"At the ranch. Offered it free and clear to Ruthann if she'd agree to sell out."

"And did she take it?"

"No. You mean Earl didn't report back to you?"

"Report back to me!" Tylson blinked, bewildered. "Hack, what are you talking about?"

"You didn't advance him that money to help you corner the Cartmell ranch?"

"You're kidding. Hand money to Earl Cartmell?"

"The stakes are high, Otto. That ranch is beautifully situated.

Whoever develops it will make millions. A man of your experience might think ten thousand was a small sum to risk. After all, every realtor around here started sniffing the wind the minute Hubert Cartmell died. Why not put up ten thousand to secure Earl's promise to sell to you and no one else? Wasn't that the deal?"

Tylson squinted at him. "You really mean this?"

"I'm asking. For Ruthann. When Hubert was dying, he told her to come to me for help in case of trouble. And she'd naturally like to know what in hell's going on. No, she didn't get straight A's in school, but she's bright enough to know Earl got that money from somebody else. And I figure that person had a lot to gain."

Tylson laughed annoyance. "Why choose me? Why not Hickman and Macaulay, why not Sunny Beach, why not—?"

"Because you're the only one fighting alongside Sharon Webb to block Ruthann's plan to save the Cartmell ranch."

"Oh, come on, Hack. You're overplaying the private detective bit. This is life, not junk television." Tylson laughed again but good-naturedly now, and shook his head in gentle toleration. Bohannon had to hand it to him. If he was guilty, he was covering it masterfully. Getting to his feet, grinning, he reached across the desk to shake Bohannon's hand. "Nice try, old friend, but no, sorry—Earl Cartmell never got any money from me."

Archie Fitzmaurice was tall, fleshy, florid-faced, and though his family had been in America for centuries, he favored rough highland tweeds, golf caps, tattersal vests, and carried a gnarled walking stick. On ceremonial occasions he'd been known to wear kilts and a tam-o'-shanter. He climbed out of his right-hand-drive 1930s Morris and marched as if to the sound of bagpipes to where Bohannon was saddling Twilight and Mousie. For a young woman and her ten-year-old daughter who stood by, the mother resigned, the child bright-eyed and so eager she couldn't stop fidgeting.

"Isn't it early for lawyers to be out?" Bohannon asked.

"Ruthann Cartmell," Fitzmaurice said, "is in trouble. She asked me to tell you."

"Give me a minute, please." Bohannon cinched the girth on Mousie, and led the two horses to the customers, saw them into the saddles, gave some words of caution and instruction, and turned back. "What kind of trouble?"

Fitzmaurice watched the woman and girl ride out the gate and start up the canyon road through the long tree shadows cast by the morning sun. "Earl is dead," he said. "Shot to death."

"I can't say I'm surprised," Bohannon said, "but it seems to me that should mean an end to Ruthann's troubles."

Fitzmaurice didn't see the humor. He shook his head. "She's been arrested. On suspicion of murder."

"No." Bohannon frowned. "Tell me about it."

"The sheriff's version? Right. Earl arrived home at midnight, she was waiting for him in the dark, and when he turned off the lights and climbed out of his car in front of the house, she shot him through the chest with one of Hubert Cartmell's rifles. His children discovered the body"—Fitzmaurice took out a pocket watch and studied it for a moment—"scarcely two hours ago. The cook, María, had shooed them out of the kitchen, and they'd run around to the front of the house to play." He tucked the watch away.

Bohannon said, "Everybody in that house hated Earl—his ex-wife Trish, even María. Why arrest Ruthann?"

"Only one rifle had been fired," Fitzmaurice said. "María cleans and shines all of them up regularly. Only the one had any fingerprints on it. And those fingerprints, unhappily, were Ruthann's."

Bohannon led the lawyer to a white slat bench near a flower bed. "What's Ruthann's explanation?"

"That the sound of a shot woke her." A bee buzzed at Fitzmaurice's ear. He absentmindedly waved it away. "She ran to the den for a gun. She went to the front door, but she was too frightened to open it." The bee buzzed at his nose. He made a slow gesture like a priestly sign of the cross. "She looked out a window, but there was no moon, it was too dark to see anything. She waited for a time, and when nothing more happened, she decided it must have been a truck backfiring down on the main road. She put the gun back in the rack, and returned to bed."

"She didn't fire the gun?"

"She says absolutely not."

"No one else heard the shot that killed Earl?"

"According to the sheriff's report—no."

"Not even Jeremy Essex?"

Fitzmaurice squinted against the bright morning sunlight. "Who's Jeremy Essex?"

Bohannon told him. "She's taken a fancy to him. I thought he might have slept over."

Fitzmaurice said, "His name isn't in the report."

Bohannon pushed up off the bench and walked across to the white fence of the paddock. Some horse had been at the top rail with its teeth. Probably Buck, back to bad old habits. He fingered the splintery place, but not thinking about it, thinking about Ruthann locked up at the sheriff station. "They sure the bullet came from that rifle?"

"The bullet went clean through him." Fitzmaurice used the walking stick to help him to his feet. Or pretended to. He wasn't an old man, or a cripple. "And they can't find it. They messed up the evidence in several ways. For one thing, they didn't look for tire tracks until they'd run three county vehicles up and down the access road and all over the ground in front of the house."

"Tire tracks?" Bohannon cocked an eyebrow.

"Someone shot the man. Lieutenant Gerard is satisfied it wasn't Trish or María, and you and I are equally sure it wasn't Ruthann. That leaves an outsider, doesn't it?" He peered into

Bohannon's face, which was shadowed by his Stetson. "Someone who arrived in a car and left in a car. Perhaps this Jeremy Essex of yours?"

"Come to think of it," Bohannon said, "he mentioned having a motel room around here. Probably on the beach."

Fitzmaurice cracked a slight smile. "Where else?"

"I know, there's a dozen," Bohannon acknowledged, "but he has a distinctive car. Italian. Red. Probably cost a hundred thousand. I'll spot it from the road."

"Unless after shooting Earl Cartmell, he left the area."

"Unless that." Bohannon nodded.

Bohannon drove the service road along the beach, slowly, studying the cars parked at each of the motels, even the cheapest. No sign of the red roadster. He hadn't time to check the motel registers. The horses wouldn't understand. He drove back up Rodd Canyon to his chores. But at the supper table, he learned what he'd feared. Rivera, who had come in the afternoon to make the beds and clean the ranch house, shook his head. "No, Hack. I'm afraid not."

With a mouthful of Stubbs's turkey stew, Bohannon blinked at him. "What do you know about it?"

Rivera didn't often smile, but now he actually grinned.

"What's up your sleeve?" Stubbs asked.

"Only what's up the sleeves of, say, fifty million other inhabitants of this great land today."

"Something on television?" Stubbs said. "You know we can't get television up here."

"This is no time for games, Manuel," Bohannon said. "A woman's life is at stake."

"Forgive me." Rivera sobered at once. "Monsignor and I had dinner last night with generous donors at their beautiful home in Santa Barbara. Mr. Lorenzin has investments in the entertainment industry. And after dinner they asked us to indulge them while they watched a television program."

Bohannon eyed him narrowly. "Which one?"

"The Grammy awards." Rivera looked questioningly at him, plainly wondering if Bohannon knew what he was talking about. Bohannon knew.

"Don't tell me," he said. "Jeremy Essex was there?"

Rivera nodded. "And not just as a spectator. He was on the stage. In front of the TV cameras. He presented several of the awards."

"And the show went on till how late?"

"Eleven," Rivera said, "though it seemed later to the poor monsignor. He kept nodding off."

"Hack, it takes four hours to drive up here from L.A.," Stubbs pointed out. "There's no way Jeremy Essex could have shot Earl Cartmell, now, is there?"

"He could have flown up, chartered a plane."

"Sorry, Hack." The *Times* lay in a disheveled stack at Rivera's elbow. He pushed it over to Bohannon. "There was a big party afterward. In Malibu. It lasted into the early hours of the morning. Essex was there. Dancing with many celebrated women. Look inside. There is a photograph."

"Forget it," Bohannon said glumly. "Essex never really figured. He wouldn't murder somebody where he planned to put on a show. Bad for business."

Bohannon drove to Fresno the next morning. The automobile showroom was deserted beyond its plate glass. Only one car stood in the wide driveway to the garage. Inside the dealership, a lone man in a business suit sat at a desk, sorting papers into a cardboard carton. The door at the side was open. Bohannon stepped in. "Excuse me?"

"Out of business," the man said without looking up.

"I didn't come for a car. I came for information."

"Sterling has folded up," the man said. "Damn good car. The Brits make great cars. But everybody wants Japanese, don't they? Shows all the good wars do."

Bohannon went to the desk. "A young fellow, very thin, very trendy clothes, bought a Sterling here in the last few days."

Bohannon took out his wallet, laid his license on the desk. "I need to find him."

The man bent his head to read the license. He had a bald spot. He looked up. "I thought the only private eyes were on TV. And you look more like you belong in westerns."

"Can you tell me the young man's name?"

The man gave back the license. "What's happened to him?"

"Something's happened to somebody he knows." Bohannon put the license away. "I need to ask him about it."

"Well," the car dealer said, smiling, rocking back in the chair, "he wouldn't be hard to remember. My last customer. Even if he hadn't paid cash."

"Whoa," Bohannon said. "That's a lot of cash, right?"

"It surprised hell out of me," the dealer said. "And if you want to know the truth, I didn't think it was his. Still, there's funny money around, you know. For big-ticket items like luxury cars. Drug money, right?" He snorted. "Even in Fresno, the raisin capital of the world."

"Drug dealers are all over. And they get younger and younger. What's his name? Where can I find him?"

"I had to do a couple things to the car to get it ready," the dealer said, "so I delivered it, so I know where he lives." He gave an address. "New condominiums."

"I don't know this town," Bohannon said. "How do I go?"

Dumping the last of the letters, receipts, computer spreadsheets into the carton, the man told him how to find the quarters of the boy whose name was not Cliff Taylor.

No one answered the doorbell. He tried the door. It opened. He went inside and closed the door. The place was handsome, still smelling of new paint, new carpeting and drapes. And something else. Unpleasant. It took Bohannon a moment to place the smell. Bleach. He went from room to room. Good furniture. Lavish electronics—forty-inch TV, VCR, stereo receiver, compact-disc player, enormous speakers. But there were signs of neglect. Videos, albums, books, magazines strewn around carelessly. A plate with a half-finished meal on it on a coffee table. A blanket tousled on the couch. And in the kitchen, what looked like a half-assed chemical laboratory. He picked up vials, bottles, jars, and set them down. A book lay open. He closed it. The cover said it contained formulae for drugs you couldn't get in the U.S., that weren't approved yet. Drugs to help you fight AIDS. He laid the book down on the counter, turned, and a wasted, bald young man with a skimpy beard was looking at him hollow-eyed from the kitchen door-way. He said, "Are you one of Dougie's friends? He never mentioned a cowboy."

"Where is he?" Bohannon said.

"The hospital," the wasted boy said, and tears began to run down his face. "He's not going to make it this time."

"Which hospital?" Bohannon asked.

And the wasted boy told him.

It was a two-bed room, and serious trouble had drawn half a dozen white-dressed nurses and green-gowned medics to one of the beds, and Bohannon waited out in the corridor. He waited standing. Down the hall was an alcove with two chairs and a sofa, but a middle-aged couple sat in the chairs, faces stiff with anxiety. Prine's parents? Four young people over-flowed the sofa. A plump rosebud of a boy, another one too thin, and a pair of manly girls, one of them in a grape-picker's straw hat. Friends of Douglas Prine's? Bohannon turned his gaze from them to the room. The door stood open. There'd be no point in closing it. Staff came and went too often and too urgently. So did equipment. The faces of the nurses, doctors, orderlies were blank, but what they felt showed in how they hurried. They were in a skirmish with an enemy that never loses. It was wonderful how they all seemed bent on winning just the same. The elevator doors at the end of the corridor opened, and five people stepped out. One of them, looking taut and pale, a bunch of plastic-wrapped flowers in his hand, was Otto Tylson. Bohannon had never seen Tylson wearing eyeglasses before; he was too vain for that. Thoughtfully, Bohannon went to meet him.

Jeremy Essex had never come to bail her out, or for any other reason, so late that afternoon, it was Bohannon who drove Ruthann Cartmell back to the ranch from the sheriff's, after the charges against her were dropped. While they rode, he talked. "Otto gave Earl that ten thousand dollars, all right. But not to secure the Cartmell ranch. It was a blackmail payoff. Earl went to Fresno now and then to play outlaw poker in some back room. He sighted Otto on the street one night with Douglas Prine, got curious, spied out what was going on, took photos, asked Otto to pay him—a couple thousand, no more. Otto paid him, but in a few weeks Earl was back, for five thousand this time. And Otto paid him again. The third time, he demanded ten thousand. Otto argued he didn't have that kind of money, but in the end he caved in and handed it over."

"And realized Earl would never stop?"

"Unless he stopped him. He couldn't get away to track Earl down, so he asked Prine to do it and then call him, when he would go wherever Earl was and kill him—though he never told Prine that part. Prine said he was too sick, so Otto sent him to hire me. I told him there was no point in looking—that Earl would go broke and come home sooner or later."

"And he did," Ruthann said wryly, "didn't he?"

"That night, Otto had worked late closing a deal and was eating at a café on the highway when he saw Earl's car heading for home. No mistaking that car. He followed it."

They drove in silence for a time. Then Ruthann sighed and said, "Poor boy," not meaning Earl.

"Otto loved him," Bohannon said. "Had for three years. Paid the rent, the bills. But while he was busy being a model citizen here by the sea, Prine was bed-hopping in the Valley. Otto knew it. He says it didn't matter. For eighteen months, Prine lied to Otto about what was wrong with him. He got away with it because Otto could only get to Fresno now and then, and never caught him at a bad time. When he finally admitted he was dying, Otto bought him a posh place to live, a fancy car, a monster television set—"

"Not life," Ruthann said. "He couldn't buy him life."

Bohannon turned off onto the access road to the ranch, and here came little Deb Cartmell, riding the horse she'd thrown stones at the other morning. He pulled the green pickup to a halt. "Howdy, cowgirl," he called.

She reined up and looked down at him. "Oh, it's you."

"You sit that horse very well," he said. "Do you have any other skills?"

She screwed her face up. "What kind of skills?"

"Ranch-hand skills, roping, shooting? Ever shoot a gun? Just for practice?"

She was wary. "What makes you think that?"

"Somebody took one of your grandfather's guns out of the rack the other day and fired it. I thought it might have been you. Just for practice." He grinned. "Hit anything?"

"A tin can on a fence post," she bragged, "first time."

"Some people are born crack shots."

"I wiped it off afterwards," she said, "like María keeps them. I didn't think anybody'd ever find out I borrowed it."

"Don't worry." He studied her, frowning. "Where'd you get the blue eye? One brown, one blue, that's unusual."

"It's a contact lens," she said. "I found it."

"Near where your father was shot?" Bohannon asked.

"How'd you know?" she said.

"It belonged to the man who killed him," Bohannon said. "Did you find anything else around there?"

She looked at him doubtfully. "Such as?"

"A bullet, maybe? In the dust?"

She complained, "How'd you get to be such a good guesser?" She sighed noisily, dug into a pocket, and tossed him a little ugly chunk of lead.

He snatched it out of the air, touched his hat brim, said, "Thank you, miss," and drove on.

"You're fantastic," Ruthann said.

Bohannon shook his head. "I haven't saved the ranch."

"You've saved my life, and where there's life there's hope." She turned him a brave smile, but they both knew she'd have to sell. In a year or two, neighborhoods would cover these rolling hills. With luck, maybe some of the oaks would stay, as reminders of the way things used to be.